FORTY-FIVE MINUTES
OF UNSTOPPABLE ROCK

Stories by
Steve Passey

FORTY-FIVE MINUTES OF UNSTOPPABLE ROCK

Stories by
Steve Passey

Tortoise Books
Chicago, IL

FIRST EDITION, NOVEMBER 2017

Published in the United States by Tortoise Books.

(www.tortoisebooks.com)

ISBN-10: 0-9986325-4-6

ISBN-13: 978-0-9986325-4-4

Praise for *Forty-Five Minutes of Unstoppable Rock*

"In Passey's stories men leave their working class jobs and their long-suffering wives behind in small towns where the desert wind makes you snap, driving off in their Impalas and El Caminos, in search of God knows what. But it's their abandoned sons and daughters that crack candy in closets, set sheds on fire, and kick dirt across a baseball diamond that shine in this car crash collection. These kids are marked, black and blue, by their hard scrabble lives. You will be, too."

- Rea Tarvydas, author of *How to Pick Up a Maid in Statue Square*

"Steve Passey's stories bring us into a world of beautiful losers: wayward, hard-luck victims of bad blood, bad judgement and bad karma. But beneath the tattoos and g-strings, almost obscured behind guns, heavy metal and El Caminos, the reader may yet discover a heart of gold or two. A little bit Raymond Carver, a little bit Cormac McCarthy and a whole lot of fun. Fasten your seat belts, it's going to be a bumpy read!"

- Lori Hahnel, author of *Love Minus Zero, Nothing Sacred* and *After You've Gone*

"Here, Steve Passey deftly paints portraits of the desperate, of those just clinging to life, those on the edge; he paints with a soft focus, letting us bear witness to their intimate moments, the aftermath of their hard decisions; here he paints in smoldering ruins."

-Robert James Russell, author of *Mesilla* and *Sea of Trees*

"I wanted to wave my lighter in the air...Here is gripping, page-turning, unflinching naturalism at its finest, with prose fine-tuned to the ugly and beautiful frequencies of the human heart. Inside the ragged bleakness of his antiheroes' lives, Passey gives us moments of transcendent beauty and grace. These are stories of innocence lost and innocence stolen – shocking, compelling, and deeply moving."

-Darrin Doyle, author, *The Dark Will End The Dark* and *The Girl Who Ate Kalamazoo*

"Steve Passey's feral imagination has produced a gripping collection of stories with compelling characters and settings evocative of small town America. The narrative is brilliantly subtle, yet brutally raw: heroes become deviants in a gritty world where common misfits and uncommon psychopaths intermingle and are almost indistinguishable amongst the mundane façades of everyday life."

-Mix Hart, author of *Queen of the Godforsaken*

Table of Contents

For Alex

Suggested Beverages

This book goes best with:

Drive-Through Coffee:

Tim's or McDonald's - Black. Only little old ladies and incestuous shut-ins drink it with cream and/or sugar. Make it black and make it hot and let's go.

Budweiser:

Anything really, as long as it's cold and in a can. "Good enough for the girls we go with" as my Granddad used to say.

Jack and Coke:

If guests are over, or under, serve them what Lemmy would have served them.

Irish Whiskey:

But make it neat. Bushmill's for one set of friends, Jameson's for the other, or Tullamore Dew and meet 'em both halfway.

Suggested Playlist:

Read this book to the suggested musical accompaniment of,

Black Dog Led Zeppelin

Never Had a Lot to Lose Cheap Trick

The Breakup Song Greg Kihn Band

Till the Next Goodbye The Rolling Stones

Bruiser Misfits

I Don't Care About You Fear

Dance the Night Away Van Halen

The River by the Garden Zeus

Paradise City Guns and Roses

All Right Now Free

Grace, Too The Tragically Hip

Bad Reputation Joan Jett

Sh Boom Life Could Be a Dream The Coasters

Repeat and Enjoy

- Steve

Tiger Lily

He took down the sign while she watched for cars. He was careful and deliberate. He had brought two small crescent wrenches and a small LED flashlight. It was his most prized possession—a gift, and he knew it was expensive. In no time at all the sign was down. He let the sign drop to the ground then jumped from the guardrail, light on his feet, and picked it back up. "Come on," he said, his voice low and quiet, and they scampered across the road, over the guardrail on the other side and then up the embankment not daring to look back.

When they got to their watching place behind some small boulders and stunted pines they sat, breathless and rasping from the short run. Her hands shaking from the effort, she brought out half a pack of cigarettes and a 40-ouncer that she had shoplifted from the convenience store in town. When he had argued against this she had advised him, in earnest, that if it wasn't worth stealing it wasn't worth having. Besides, she supported the place by buying cigarettes, and they owed her. An empty 40, dirty and half-crushed, was wedged between two of the rocks. There were some cigarette butts against the base of the pine where the wind allowed them to settle after curling over the boulders and around the tree before gathering momentum and scouring the more exposed areas of the hillside.

"That bottle is bigger than you are," he said with admiration. She smiled and lit a cigarette, still catching her breath. She waved her hand in a circular motion, and he watched, waiting for explanation.

"Are you sure you have never taken anyone else here before?" she asked and coughed. She gestured at the discarded 40 and the butts.

"No," he said. "No. You are the first. That shit is all mine. You can spend quite a bit of time up here waiting." He did not look at her when he spoke, and stared down at the road instead. When he finally turned to her he smiled and said "I didn't know it was gonna kill you to run up this far. I mean, man, all across the road and 50 feet up a hill? What was I thinking?"

She laughed, then coughed and spat. "Asshole! You never said anything about running!" A smile and a couple of deep drags on the cigarette and her breathing returned to normal.

He looked her over without expression. She had taken off her jacket and exposed her bare arms. She was wearing a black halter top. She wore jeans and canvas running shoes, high-tops with rubber soles, Chuck Taylors. One of her stepfathers had found them. He was a physically strong man and had lifted weights. She had never asked him (or any of the other stepfathers) for anything other than to be left alone. He had bought them for her and for that she remembered him, a strong man generous with sneakers.

She had white, white skin, with a month-old tattoo of a tiger lily, orange and green and beautiful on her left shoulder. He liked girls who tattooed their arms, and not an ankle or the small of their back or their bikini line, tattooed with some tiny Japanese lettering that they did not understand, or some tribal latticework that no one would ever see—things that meant nothing to them. Those were tattoos bought because everyone else was getting one. They were the ornamentation of the moment, but told no story. A *real* tattoo tells a story and fades only reluctantly, when the memory of the event that inspired it becomes obscure. A story is the soul of a tattoo. Tattoos without a story have no soul and fade away to look like a bruise. She wanted full sleeves, both arms tattooed shoulder to wrist, and they had read through tattoo magazines many times picking just this one or that. He liked black and gray art and skulls, but she wanted color and for her first tattoo she had gotten the tiger lily. He now thought that she had made the right choice. Her lower lip was pierced as well, the little stainless steel stud highlighting her facial symmetry. In this, too, she had been right. He had thought that she should get her lip pierced with a ring, off-center. She had listened to him without comment each time he had debated it but he was debating with himself because when she did it she went and did it her way.

Her hair was dark brown; so dark she called it black. It was ferocious and wavy and not dyed. She hated it of course, and grew it long hoping its own weight would tame it but it only grew even wilder. Everyone else loved it. She had those faux cats-eye glasses that she didn't need to read and generally wore perched up on top of her head, which was to both of their esthetic senses an affectation, but it was an affectation she liked. He had mocked her for it but she would not give up the glasses nor stop perching them atop her feral hair.

"Tell me again why you got the lily," he said, reaching over to run his thumb on the embossed image upon her pale skin.

"I've told you a hundred times already," she said, without sounding angry or impatient. She was beginning to turn quiet, the nicotine had seeped in, and the first swallows from the 40, warmish and bitter, had mellowed her.

"Tell me again then," he repeated, "I like the story. It makes me feel all warm inside."

She laughed, genuinely this time, without coughing.

"Ok, Mr. Big Idiot. Here it is. My dad—my real dad, not any of those other guys my mom attaches us to on her bad days—always called me Tiger Lily when I was a baby. I can remember him calling me Tiger Lily when I was like two or three. I was so small I couldn't count but I could hear and I can remember it—So poo on you if you want to argue. Now, when he calls me—on every Christmas Eve and every birthday—he calls me Tiger Lily. And I like it, so there!"

He had argued that with her before, saying that she had made up the memory because she had wanted it. She had stuck to her story, that the memory was real and true, and finally had told him that even if she had made it up it was her very own imaginary memory and she was keeping it. There are only two ways to argue with a woman and neither of them works, so he had conceded her the story. Truthfully, he did like the story, just like he liked the story about the shoes.

"Are we going to see an accident soon?" she asked.

He straightened up and looked over the embankment. "Can't say for sure," he said. "Never can. There isn't much traffic up here on a Friday night. Just listen. It's quiet up here and we'll hear a car before we see it. With the sign down they won't slow down or see the s-curve. Most times all you get is squealing tires, especially from those old piece-of-shit pickups all the rednecks in this shit-hole drive, but once in a while someone in a hot car going too fast will come up and do a three-sixty."

"Yes, but—do you think we'll see one?" she asked again, and then lowering her tone to confessional "Broken chrome and shattered glass?"

"I hope so," he said. "I mean, that's what we're here for. That's why I got the sign."

They sat quietly, smoking cigarettes and sipping cheap malt. At this latitude the sun does go down on a hot summer night, but you can see the pale blue glow of pre-dawn in the sunset almost until the point when the same blue glow appears pre-dawn in the east. So they sat on the hillside and waited, their eyes intent upon the road, and in turn watched over by the firmament above them. They did not need to fend of sleep; anticipation was enough to keep them awake.

"Listen," he said, "do you hear? Car!"

She sat still, extra still, holding the warm 40 between both hands and hunching over to keep it still. She had to fight the urge to stand and crane her neck out over the boulders. He had warned her she could be seen if she did that.

"No, it's nothing," he said after a minute, and the tension seeped out and relaxed into the ground. The night was still very warm and she had not put her jacket back on. There was no moon so the planet Venus was the brightest object in the sky. Venus is bright enough at some latitudes to cast a shadow, and on this night the light of Venus on her porcelain skin was enough to see the tiger lily.

He sat and watched her and could see that she had become very tired and could feel the irresistible pull towards sleep that mountain air and starlight exerted upon her.

"Ok. What do you do when there is a wreck?" he demanded, trying to rouse her from her reverie.

She closed her eyes and repeated her mantra: "Do not stand up. Do not go down. Wait, and watch. The magic is in the moment; don't intrude." Her voice was clear, and he could tell that his question had brought her back to him.

"And what do you do when there is an accident?" she asked, engaging him in the same way.

"Don't worry about me," he said softly, "I know what to do."

"Tell me again," she cooed. "You know I like the story." Her eyes were still closed, She was leaning back upon her elbows, and the midnight light of Venus made her a creature of shadow and silver silhouette.

Softly again, softly, "I have to take the sign back and get it back up. I have 30 seconds to do this. In this time no one from the accident will be able to see me—they will have other things to worry about. Any vehicles following the scene are unlikely to see me, because they have other things to look at."

She paused there, the silhouette of Venus, and was breathing so quietly he could not hear her. For a short time but a long moment they sat in this silence, so long that they each felt the precession of the heavens whose measurement was until recently beyond the life span of any one person. The movement of the heavens was a thing felt before it was observed; the ancients found it because they were compelled to look for it by the very core of their being. It is the argument from design. Precession is the pull of gravity upon the soul. With the understanding of precession, time was deciphered into quantity and removed from the realm of the soul into that of the intellect. Someday, we will control time, and when we can do that we will miss it from when it was free and our master. Moments however, moments remain observed only by the spirit and remain forever in the domain of the esthetic, the property of prophets and goddesses.

"I was in a car accident once," she finally spoke. "I mean, it was nothing. We were rear-ended by an old lady in the hardware store parking lot. It was funny, she got out and was all like apologetic at first, but then she got madder and madder. She did not yell or point fingers, and I forget exactly how she put it, but she more or less wanted the accident to be our fault. What were *we* doing there, at *that* particular spot, at *that* particular time? Like I said, I forget what she said exactly, but what she meant was that because there were the two of us there at that time we were at least partially to blame."

"Like it was meant to be?" he asked, long after she had lapsed back into silence. She was lying on her right side, on the tiger lily, and he could not see it.

"Hell no!" She drawled out the profanity, dragged it out into sarcasm. "Mom got a lawyer. We got a cool ten thousand for our pain and suffering from the old lady's insurance company. The lawyer kept four thousand for his time and his pain and suffering I guess—the fucker—but you know how my mom is. She gave most of it up to a boyfriend she had. He spent it all on VLTs. She hid a little and we moved out here on it."

"Just like it was meant to be," he said. He had not moved, not lied down the whole time. He sat with his back against one of the boulders, his knees up against his chest and he smoked slowly and cautiously like an old man and passed the warm 40. He did not close his eyes or doze off. He looked at her, at Venus, and at the lesser stars of the night sky, but mostly he listened for the sounds of an approaching vehicle.

"That's not much of a car accident," he said quietly, almost to himself.

She rolled over on her side, the tiger lily up to look at Venus, all shoulders and hips and wavy black hair. Her skin was almost blue in the light. There are goddesses older than Venus, these old blue goddesses of the Mediterranean. Their hair matted with the memory of Medusa and her serpentine locks and the demand for sacrifice.

"Have I ever been in a car accident? Oh yeah. That's why I am here. Not a fender-bender on the ice in a parking lot, but in one 'at speed.' You would think that your life would flash before your eyes and that you would be afraid to die, but the truth is you are not. It happens too fast. You are the observer who blinks and misses. The noise, the noise—that sound will bring you back to the accident when you try to remember it. BANG! Like being in the barrel of a gun when the hammer comes down. BANG! An accident is a contest between gravity and momentum, and in that second when momentum holds sway you are pulled in a thousand different directions. It's like falling. You fall off your body and out of your mind. It's just physics—cold and impersonal—and to stand against it we all hope we have a soul because our bodies must give way. It's falling off of a mile-high cliff but with a lottery ticket's chance at a better outcome. When gravity wins as it must you will lie there unsure if you are still you or not. You will forget everything. You will be nameless. Then the adrenaline will surge and you will feel cold, like being naked in the snow. The cold is in your spine and on the backs of your arms. You might laugh, a thin hiccup of a laugh, and then if you are to die you will grow colder and might cry. But you are only thinking of crying because when they find you, there will be no tears upon your dead face. Your soul remembers the emotion for a brief second after your body is unable to continue the process. If you live, you will soon be conscious of blood and broken glass, even before you remember your name. If you are going to live, adrenaline and pain will tell you soon enough. You will look up at the sky and see the stars. Maybe then you will see your own mortality, not as your life passing before your eyes but as the tiniest precessional sliver of time that is your life when set against the stars. You sleep on pavement or on gravel— lucky for you if it is grass—but no bed of rest is too uncomfortable now. That's the hormones holding you up and away. I imagine that to die is to become part of the ground. To live is to be part of the wind. Soon enough the witnesses can come. No one will have seen the moment of impact, when gravity and momentum fought, but they will have heard the crash and one brave person will come running. The rest will walk. Perhaps it will be a woman, motherly like Mary, with a blanket and a hand upon your forehead asking, "Are you all right?"

"Were you all right?" She asked, wide-eyed and admiring.

"All right? Better than all right. More like fuckin' Superman."

"I love it when you talk like that. That's why I came. I don't care anymore about seeing one."

He was quiet again, lost in thoughts of broken glass. When he looked up again he could see that the thin light left by the sunset had circled the pole and was now coming from the promise of sunrise a few hours away.

"Time to go," he said softly. "There won't be an accident tonight. It's after 2 a.m. and even all the drunks will find their way home without using this road. I'm sorry it didn't work out."

There are three memes people have when apologizing. The first one they use when they lie and they are not sorry at all, but must observe the formality of apology to satisfy a social obligation. The second they use when they apologize truly and deeply and too late. There, they submit themselves and ask for absolution from the wronged. This is rare. The third is when they apologize for something that is not their fault, for the discourtesy of nature or of circumstance. We apologize to our children and to our loved ones like this, on those moments when their lives are disappointed. This is no apology of course; by definition you hold no fault and owe no debt. It is solace, and of all apologies it is the most sincere.

He picked up the sign and moved carefully down the hillside, slowly now, with no need to run. She followed carefully, carrying the empty 40 full of butts and still conscious of the wheezing induced by her sprint up the hill earlier. He balanced on the guardrail easily, and with the tools in his hands and the LED light in his mouth had the sign back up again in as little time as it took to take it down.

"Maybe next time," she said, thinking of the BANG and blood and chrome.

"If you look around you can see bits of glass and a few pieces of this and that from the last one," he told her. "It's like being in a cemetery, but different. I believe that certain objects retain the memory of the people attached to them. Tonight this is enough for me."

She didn't bother to look; she was too tired now to be bothered looking for the relics of wrecks. They began to walk back into town. She was quiet, and with the pre-dawn light and Venus setting she no longer had the ghostly outline she had had up on the hill beneath the ragged pines. She wore her jacket and the tiger lily slept beneath it on its bed of porcelain skin.

"Tell me the story again, Tiger Lily."

"No. Enough already, I'm really tired."

"Can I call you Tiger Lily, Tiger Lily?"

"Nope. Only my dad."

"Tiger Lily," he said to himself. "Blue Venus."

The River by the Garden

Stone from the quarry comes down to our shop and is made into monuments. You can see them in the cemetery behind the church, behind Jesus in his house under his father's roof. There are rows of stones there with consecutive dates that tell of some catastrophe born of high water, and here and there a small group with a common surname and a singular date, a calamity made from fire.

Friday after work the boys get together for a shop party. Some days in August it's just too hot and humid to go home. We sit in the shop with the doors open, have a few beers, and try to catch a breeze. Little drops of condensation form on the cans and it goes down like manna from heaven.

Cheesey is there complaining about his friend's car. His real name is Kenny, but everyone calls him Cheesey. The nickname has stuck with him so long no one remembers how he got it.

"Saddest thing I ever heard," Cheesey said. "My buddy is sitting there in lockup on account of he sold a one-hitter to an undercover cop. A one-hitter! Everyone knows he ain't a dealer. He was just being sociable. So he pled guilty just to get past it. But the state fined him, fined him hard. They gave him two years' probation, and seized his El Camino as 'The proceeds of crime.' He's a working man like all of us, he spent eight years fixing it up, and all of a sudden it's 'the proceeds of crime?'"

We all nod except for Wilkie. Wilkie isn't at the shop often, just on the hottest days. He's been at the quarry for twenty years now and the dust from working stone has gotten into his hands. His palms are as white as an alabaster Christ, like the Christ up there above the altar in the church, Jesus who looks down with pity at all of us.

He spoke quietly, almost to himself: "Back in '93 when it rained a whole month and the levees started to break I was sandbagging like everyone else. We filled those bags and stacked 'em up. The rain clouds finally busted up and went away but we still bagged until last light. At about the same time our backs and shoulders all gave out and we stood there, bent over and breathing hard, watching that dirty river roll on by. Things come on down the river. The roofs of houses, the sides of barns, dead cows and living trees. By light of the setting sun, I saw a baby's coffin on the river, all by itself.

"I saw that little coffin go by, white with a gold cross upon it, and I thought for a moment it must be my baby brother Jimmy. I never did know him. He was born with a hole in his heart and they couldn't fix it. He had the surgery and then he passed. My momma still carries that with her. I hadn't thought of Jimmy in years but when that baby's coffin come by, small and white as it was, I thought right away it had to be Jimmy."

No one spoke. Everyone just looked at the ground or at each other. Wilkie continued:

"It's a hard thing only when it's hard on the living and the dead. A vehicle is just tin. I'll tell you what: The State will auction off that El Camino next month. Your friend can just go on and buy it back. Ain't no one who knows him gonna bid against him. It won't cost him any more than the fine did."

"Yeah, he could do that," said Cheesey. "He could, all right. If he wanted."

Cooler now, finally. A breeze is coming down through the trees and through the quiet, born from the clouds of a distant storm way up across the river. It brings relief from the clinging dust and is a balm against the heat.

Flower

Flower had been there first. Flower was four years old; the baby was two. Flower was a Shepherd-Rottie cross. The baby had the blondest hair as fine as corn silk. She had hardly started to walk before she began to run. Everyone loved her.

In the yard, the barbecue smoked and the music played in the late afternoon sun. The baby laughed and ran. "FLOWER, NO!" the baby's mother had shouted, her voice high and thin. "FLOWER, NO!" sharp and hard. Flower had not even barked but she had taken the baby into her mouth by the neck and shaken her, shaken her hard and flung her to the ground with the sound of a wet towel snapping. "FLOWER, NO!"

Flower had cowered before the baby's mother and offered her belly. "FLOWER, WHAT HAVE YOU DONE!" the mother wept, cupping the dog's face in her shaking hands. The mother's boyfriend had come running with a shovel. "NO!"

the mother said, but she was too late and Flower yelped with the first blow and then howled and ran at the second. The blows sounded like raw meat dropping on pavement. A third caught her and cut her on her hindquarters but she kept her feet on the ground and ran down the street screaming like a burning thing.

That was the last anyone on the lawn saw her—the mother, the baby, the boyfriend. Anyone. Anyone except the municipal officials who caught her and the vet who put her down.

The baby lay on the lawn, already sublimated to the earth. She lay there resting her head on a silky halo, her blue eyes looking towards bright sky, breathing but not moving. The mother knelt over her, knelt over her and wrung her hands, her tears, her prayers.

The ambulance came within minutes.

Baby needed eighty-one stitches. Baby lay twenty-nine days in the hospital's care. She was assessed to be "cognitively impaired."

"What is that?" the mother asked, "What is that?"

That was followed by thirty days in the custody of Children's Services.

"Why that?" the mother asked, "Why that?"

In due course Baby was returned to her mother. Baby did not talk. She did not walk. No one could speak of the days when she ran. Everyone still loved her.

"We will do what we can," they said.

"There is no looking back, only forward," they added.

"Attitude is everything," they hoped.

These were their mantras; these were their prayers.

The mother took her child outside for fresh air. She'd lie upon the silken crown of her hair and stare at the sky. The mother would take her inside. She would lie there resting her head upon that same hair and stare at the ceiling with the same eyes. And so the days passed, one the same as the other except for those days when the cognitive impairment would cast a shadow and the baby—a child now but hair still fine and eyes still blue—would pitch a fit. A hum would become a moan; a moan would become a scream. The scream would become another scream and the world would stop for an hour while she screamed and screamed and screamed. The mother would pick her up and hold her too tightly and rock and rock and rock and her tears were her prayers. Her prayers would fall upon her child's face and she'd rest, the girl in her lap and her back against the wall. She would hold the child's face against hers and every time she did she thought she could smell the breath of her dog on the face of her daughter.

Always then, always with the salt of her tears mixing with the breath of the dog the child would cease to scream. She'd sleep then, closing her eyes so blue, her fine hair damp with sweat.

"Flower," the mother would say, her eyes on the ceiling, or even on the sky. "Flower."

"Flower."

One Inch of Air

When the ice freezes on the lake, freezes fast and hard, there will be almost one inch of air between the bottom of the ice and the water below.

Twenty years ago, Mike and I were out on our snowmobiles on the last day of February, hauling ass before the sunset. The first warm breath of spring had come in hard from the southwest and we were out in jeans and T-shirts and our felt-lined boots with neckerchiefs of red and blue worn over our mouths and necks. We were cowboys on sleds and we rode like hell. We raced across the lake at the narrow end, the deep end. My sled carried a little air off of the bank and I hit the ice first. Her rear end wanted to come around, but I feathered the throttle, used a little body English, and shot across the lake, blinded by the setting sun with a full moon coming up at my back. There were already geese in the sky. I looked over my shoulder for Mike and I saw his sled disappear through the ice. It slipped through a crack that I must have made when I landed; it nosed up and slid backwards, fast. The crack chased me and ice came up from where Mike went down in handfuls of edges while I slowed down.

I ride to the far bank and get off with the motor still running.

I climb up the bank, towards a lone poplar tree asleep in winter, and break off a long branch. The branch is dead in my hands with winter in its veins. The poplars have a wisdom of their own—a life, a soul, beyond that of the lake and the ice. Their sap doesn't run with a warm wind but with the hours of sunlight that come with the solstice. This way they don't leaf out too early and die in a late frost. They mark time by the stars. I believe that to be conscious of time is the essence of being. The poplar can understand time, and so has a soul. The snow, the ice, the lake—it's all just chemistry. Water has no soul.

I never say a word. I don't yell. I don't cry. I guess that I have a minute and know the setting sun will tell me when time runs out. I run, run my mouth dry with fear at the sound of my own boots on the ice, waiting for the telltale crack to tell me that it is giving chase. I run back onto the lake for as far as I dare run, I walk as far as I dare walk, and then I lie on my belly and slide as close to the hole as I dare slide. I hold the branch out to the hole where Mike has gone down. I am brave and pathetic at the same time, craven on my belly. I imagine him falling backwards off the sled, falling away, and in that moment I imagine myself in the water as if I am Mike. I can taste the cold water in my mouth, and feel the shock of it coming over me. Cold water, really cold, has a weight to it. It's like an anvil sitting on your chest and you cannot draw breath. I get the branch over the hole and then I start yelling for Mike, yelling as loud as I can, wide-eyed and hoarse with fear. "Mike!" I yell, "Mike buddy! Can you hear me? Can you hear me?" I am wild-eyed, shouting and crazy, a man who has killed his friend. The sun is gone and the moon sheds enough light to expose me, but not enough to find Mike. "Mike," I cry to the moon, "Mike," I whisper to the ice. "Mike," I think to myself, "I can't get any closer."

Ten feet from where Mike went in, I stop.

I close my eyes and the cold seeps into me until it becomes warmth. The branch hits the water and I let go, let it go and feel it slide into the blue black of the lake in late winter. The lake thought it might be spring.

I close my eyes.

Divers found Mike's sled. They never found Mike. He is underneath the water. "That lake doesn't give up its dead," people said. "Deep and cold year round. No oxygen." Some spoke of crevasses at the bottom, dark and cold, where rivers ran before there were people, before there was a lake.

I walked the shoreline in summer, the poplars full with leaves, and their sap dripping like sweat. Once—just this once—on some rushes far away from where Mike had fallen away beneath the ice, I saw something in a red-winged blackbird's nest. I thought it was a piece of felt from Mike's boots. I walked into the rushes but it was too far away. I waded out until the water was past my waist but I could not see. The rushes were over my head and I lost sight of the nest in their sway. When my feet could no longer touch the bottom, I had to swim, but with the rushes so high I lost even the shore and I floated on back under the sun until I could think again. I floated on a current I hardly noticed until my feet found the bottom and I waded back up to the bank and finally walked up on dry land. Nothing was familiar. Even though I tried and tried I could not retrace my steps to the spot where I had first seen the blackbird's nest and it was lost to me. Who knows? Maybe the wind had taken it or I had been seeing things. These are the things I tell myself. These are things I do not believe. I close my eyes and I can see the felt in the blackbird's nest.

A fisherman found Mike's watch. This was in July; fourteen years after Mike had disappeared. He had this watch his mother gave him when he was ten. It was his grandfather's watch—her father's—and Mike was named for him and their name was engraved on the watch. Mike always called it his grandfather's watch. The fisherman was looking for pike: a terrible fish that can grow to be as long as man is tall and as thick as a man's leg. Rows of teeth. Pike that big don't fight, they sink into the darkness and hold onto the shadows and wait you out. He had cast a line with a heavy weight and one of those three-tined hooks that look like an anchor and he had drawn it back and the watch came out. He gave it to the Fish & Wildlife guys, and one of them brought it to Mike's mom and she held it and said nothing, not knowing where to put it but not wanting to set it down.

I open my eyes.

I open my eyes at the sound of ice cracking and there below me is Mike. He has come to the surface from the other side only feet away from where he had gone in. Strange, this mirror of ice and air between us. Strange, his hands flat with his palms pressed to mine from his side. Strange, now in the one inch of air beneath me, his face. He is white now, so white he shines, he glows, his pupils so wide they almost eclipse his irises. He looks at me with wonder in this one inch of air and his mouth moves as if to speak but his pupils grow small and he sinks away into the water below me and becomes invisible. The last thing I see is the glint of his watch before all is darkness. My mouth open, now I am screaming against ice and I taste the brine of the lake. I back away, the ice cracking in little spider web cracks beneath me, and I slink on my belly until my boots gain the bank and I get up and run to my sled and fly into town. It takes two hours for search and rescue to get there. The divers go in the next day.

Once in town, I saw a small child pick up a penny and smile. He could not have imagined that I saw him, watched him stand up surprised and pleased with his luck, his possession of a secret that is of a particular moment. What do children see? It's a mystery to me. I have seen that face before in winter, seen it in water. I am reminded of a thing, the thing, with Mike in the water.

I still come out here sometimes. I come in high summer where I scan the rushes and the blackbird's nests. I come in the dead of winter when it's thirty below and the moon makes the ice crystals in the air sparkle and dance like familiar spirits.

I once heard two old guys talking about the color of the ice and how it will tell you if it is safe to walk on. I walked away before I heard them describe that color. I wonder if I will know it when I see it, the next time I go out. I saw that child with his penny and saw how he sought it out from a glint of sunlight on copper. It is the smallest thing. It reminds me of a flash of metal in the water underneath a shifting sky, and of the souls of trees, and of false springs and the crack of ice falling into one inch of air.

I will know it when I hear it.

Black Dog

Old Man Solomon has a dog with some Blue Heeler in him, low and mean. You have to keep your head on a swivel with that dog around. Like all Blue Heelers, it will bite, and like all Blue Heelers, it won't bark. No warning, just teeth. My twin sister Jenny and I will walk past the old man's place on the other side of the street, like Momma told us to do, rather than get on the dog's side. Some parents complain to the old man, either call him up or talk across the fence when they see him in his yard. "Keep that dog off of our kids," they say, and he always comes back with "Keep them kids outta my yard." No one was ever in his yard, but he knew it was some kid's word vs. his. He never even gave the dog a name. Imagine that. He never named his dog. Once in a while the bylaw officer would drive by, but he never did catch the dog out of the yard. I saw that dog bite a kid once. Walked up behind him with his head low and went right at the kid's ankle, right at the tendon, just a quick nip. The kid yelped and turned around and the Blue Heeler with no name stood there without a sound, with his head low, his eyes up, his teeth bared and the hair on his back standing up. You have to keep your eye on that dog.

***

"Jenny," I said, "It's about a girl."

"Heidi Weller," she said. There are few things that surprise my sister. And we are twins.

"Heidi Weller," I said. "I want to ask her to dance at the dance."

"So ask her," Jenny says.

"I can't unless I know for sure she's not going to say no."

"Well, I can't ask her for you. I am not friends with her," Jenny said "She's a rich kid. Besides, just like *you* find it easier to ask me to ask her so you can know ahead of time, she will find it easier to say no to me in order to say no to *you* ahead of time."

"Are you saying she won't dance with me?" I asked, knowing this is the lesser of two evils. Better to hear it here and now than to experience it in front of the whole school.

"Don't put words in my mouth," Jenny said. "What I am saying is that you are going to have to ask her to find out. If *I* ask her she will *probably* say no. But if *you* ask her at the dance she will *probably* say yes. That's as good of advice as I can give you. You're thirteen, Danny—some things you are just going to have to do on your own."

I think for a minute. "I wonder if Clayton would help?"

Jenny just looks at me. This is her soft spot. Clayton's momma works at the call center with ours. They live in a trailer a block over, past Old Man Solomon's place. Jenny has had a crush on Clayton forever. Clayton used to party his ass off. He did not give a single, solitary shit about anything. She liked him for that. Then he decided to get serious so he could get into the service. He cut his hair, got a job, and started to give a shit about a few things. She liked him even more for that. Clayton used to babysit us back in his hair days when our moms would go out with people from work on Fridays. It was cool as shit. We'd play video games, drink cokes non-stop, and crank up the tunes.

"He might," Jenny said slowly. "Like I said, you gotta ask yourself."

A few months ago, Mom had taken me to visit our dad's parents. We didn't see them often and Jenny refused to go. I'm not sure of the right or wrong of that. But she stayed home and we went. When I got back, Jenny was kind of quiet. Not sad-quiet—just quiet-quiet. I thought she might be hiding something. I brought it up and she just looked at me like I was stupid. It drove me crazy to the point I had to be direct with her. Finally—finally—after a week when Mom wasn't around, I cornered her in her room and asked her point blank "Did you try weed?"

This was our thing. We are twins. When we were ten or eleven, we had decided that we would maybe someday—maybe—try weed, but not without each other. We are twins. We'd do this thing together or not at all. I was pretty much convinced. Jenny just looked at me.

"No." she said. "Anyway, I had forgotten all about that. How do you even remember such things?" By now I was totally convinced she had smoked weed.

"I'm telling Mom you smoked weed," I said. "Pothead!" I hissed. It was all I could think of to say.

"Don't you dare!" she shrieked.

"Either you tell me what you did or I'm telling Mom you smoked weed," I spat back.

"Ok," she said "But I'm telling you only because we're twins. You remember that time when you went off to see Dad's parents and I stayed home alone?"

I nodded.

"Clayton came over. We just hung out. It was nice. Just two friends, just hanging out."

"And smoking weed!" I said, "Like you'd be all off in La-La Land like you are and not tell me for a week that Clayton came over. That's no big deal. That's nothing at all."

She looked at me for a long time then, just looked. Weighing and measuring. "Get into my closet," she finally said, looking close at me the whole time. She went to her dresser and brought out a roll of those hard candy breath mints with the little sparkles in them. She got into the closet with me and shut the door. It was dark in there and warm, and smelled of her clean clothes that Momma had laundered.

"Look at my mouth," she said, and I looked where I thought her mouth was. I could hear her unwrap the breath mints with her hand and then feel her move her hand up to put it her mouth. I could smell it briefly on her lips and then hear it on her tongue as she rolled it in her mouth and clicked it on her teeth. She was quiet for a moment and then—*CRACK*—she bit down hard and tiny sparks shot into the closet from her mouth and her breath was heavy and sweet and I am sure I smiled with an open mouth.

"How did you do that?" I asked.

"It's called sparking," she said, "It's easy. You take the hard candy, put it on your back teeth so that it lies up and down and not flat and then all at once, you bite down hard and fast and crush it. Pop! Little sparks from it, fly out of your mouth. Don't suck on it—it needs to be pretty dry. Remember to keep your mouth open."

She pressed a Cert into my hand and I popped it into my mouth and did as she said and she laughed out loud. "It worked perfectly!"

she said, and then we went through the pack of mints, each in turn, until there were none.

"So this is what you did with Clayton?" I asked when we were done, before we left the closet.

"Sparking," she said in a stage whisper, and opened the door. The light from outside was too bright then, and I closed my eyes, and the last thing I saw was the dust motes in the air just barley moving, as if they were too tired or maybe just lazy from the heat to coalesce into something other than what they were.

I started walking over to Clayton's place with my head full of Heidi Weller. Heidi was blonde: not as blonde as she had been when we were in grade school when her hair was practically white, but blonde the color of honey and cinnamon, and she had brown eyes. She wore white shirts. She wore dresses. She played volleyball and wore makeup and her daddy was rich. She had a lot of friends. Next week would be the last week of school before summer break, and there would be a dance. I so wanted to dance with Heidi Weller. In that brief shining moment, I'd be somebody—no doubt about it. She had a lot of friends. I just wanted to dance with her but while I was walking, I thought I might like to go sparking with her, too, and I thought about her in the dark of my sister's closet and I shook my head and opened my eyes and tried to walk faster but I closed them again and she was in the closet and I saw her dark against the golden dust motes and heard a *crack* from her mouth and I saw the little sparks fly and I imagined her mouth to be soft and her breath to smell of candy and strawberry lip gloss. I kept my eyes closed even while I walked and I walked so slowly, I might as well have been standing. I didn't know why I imagined strawberry lip-gloss. I just imagined that it has to be nice.

Old Man Solomon's nameless dog bit me right about then—hard and quick—right on the back of the ankle, right on the tendon. It hurt like hell and I fell down. I was scared of the fucking dog but just as mad, too—the little bastard just circumcised my dream of Heidi Weller's strawberry lip-gloss and sparking in my twin sister's closet. I got up like a white-hot shot and faced off with the nameless spotted devil. Him with his head low and teeth bared without a sound and me backing up, limping and waving both arms, hurling a steady stream of F-bombs at him with the spit and hate flying from my mouth. I was loud enough for both of us—even for all of us kids who ever got bit by that dog—if words had weight, I'd have crushed him to a blue stain. I walked backwards up to Clayton's a half block away. He turned his back and went back into Old Man Solomon's yard and I turned and walked up to Clayton's Momma's trailer door and knocked.

Clayton opened the door and offered a fist bump. "Bro," he said, "why the limp?"

"Fucking Old Man Solomon's dog bit me," I said.

"Ah Bro-ski," he said, "You didn't go the long way around did you? Mind you, you shouldn't have to."

I just nodded. The fear was gone; my mouth was so dry. My ankle still hurt.

"I'll tell you what," Clayton said, "Let's fix that dog for you. I'm sick of that bullshit. Old Man Solomon will be in the city today—drinking at the VFW—he won't be back until supper. Everyone else here is at work. Let's fix that dog."

I shrugged my shoulders and nodded. My ankle felt better already.

Clayton wasn't wearing a shirt; he never did now. Since he cut his hair and got that job at the drilling mud place he never wore a shirt. Just jeans and those steel-toed cowboy boots he got for work. You could see the veins in his biceps now, the triangle of his shoulder muscles, and he had abs. Clayton was always showing a six.

"Gotta get in shape for the service," he told me once, and patted his abs. I looked away. It seemed kind of weird to admire his abs. He got them loading bags of drilling mud onto pallets. Labor looks good on a young man.

Clayton and his abs pulled on his steel-toed boots, walked on out into the first hot day of summer and started looking around the trailer.

He pulled up an old two-by-four, five feet long, splintered at one end with nails sticking out of the other, and swung it in a wide arc like a baseball bat and then overhand, more straight up-and-down, like a hammer. The board had faded to gray with age and he set it down without saying anything. He went under the steps and fished out an old propane barbecue tank, more rust than silver paint on it, and swung that around a little, too.

"Ugh," he said. "Too heavy," and set it back down under the steps. He walked back down to the back corner of the trailer near the gas meter and pulled out a rusty iron bar that was lying by the trailer—rebar actually, the kind of rod used to reinforce concrete. It was rusty with age but made a happy whipping sound when he swung it. Long enough to reach a dog, I thought, light enough to swing, and easy enough to keep a hold of.

"Found this when I was six," he said. "Stuck it in a fire ant's nest once. Ran like hell. Glad I kept it. Glad Momma didn't find it and throw it away. It'll do. Now let's go show that damn dog who's boss."

We walked down the street together and then turned to go past Old Man Solomon's. He stopped there and said, "Tell you what, go on a head of me—ten steps. Keep your eye out for that dog. When he comes out behind you like he does, you stare him down. I'll come up behind him and fuck his shit up with the rebar."

I nodded and walked on ahead. Briefly, briefly, I thought of Heidi Weller in a blue summer dress, her hair in a single braid, her brown eyes flashing. I almost laughed, and I am sure I blushed but in the same second, I remembered that I was afraid of the dog. I forgot to count to ten. Where was the dog? Where? I looked behind me and sure enough, there he was, coming in low. He was all black on his back and his hackles were up, his sides the mottled gray of one of those World War II German fighter planes. His eyes were more orange than brown, and in the curl of his lip, his teeth were bare and he made no sound at all.

I stood there, my palms out and my fingers up, eye-to-eye with the devil, and heard Clayton's steel-toed boots coming up fast like a hammer striking metal and saw in the early afternoon sun the arc of the rebar in Clayton's hands as it came down at the nameless dog, the rebar descending as if from a great height. *Crack!* it went, across the black back, and the dog screamed—a shriek that could break glass— and the dog was on his side, his paws moving like he was swimming, and I laughed out loud. Clayton brought the bar down a second time, harder now; he had reached so far behind him to generate momentum, the bar scraped on the concrete of the sidewalk before he brought it up and over and it came around, came over, came to the dog with a deeper, harder *CRACK!* and the black dog shrieked again—so loud now I had to look around. He was almost totally over on his back now, his paws in the air as if to protect his face, not unlike me with my own hands a moment ago. Clayton took the rebar for the third time and, holding it by one end in both hands, he drove it straight down through the dog's belly like a sword, like a marker, like a period at the end of sentence. The rebar went through the fur on the dog's belly, gray and soft and sparse, and through him. There was a muted *chunk* sound as the point of the rebar reached the other side of the dog and hit the concrete of the sidewalk beneath it. The dog made a sound like air leaving a ball: a long and sharp series of breaths like *HAHAHAHAHAHA!* They rattled down the street and up past the tree leaves into a cloudless sky and Clayton and I stood there with our hands empty and stared at the dog. We were breathing hard and our palms were sweaty and the dog lied sort of on its back and on its side with almost 2 feet of rebar pointing straight up.

No one moved until Clayton stepped forward and spit on the dog, phlegm white and heavy, and said, "Not so tough now are you, you little motherfucker."

He held out his fist to me for a fist bump and I touched my fist to his, just barely touched it, my eyes on the rattling dog at our feet.

The dog rolled onto his belly then, the rebar falling over to hit the concrete with another, sharper *chunk,* this one not muted by his own body. His jaws opened in a rictus of a grin and his eyes so wide open you could see the whites. His eyes rolled, orange and white, but he would not look at us. Clayton pushed the dog's hindquarters with the toe of his boot and said, "Look at me, you motherfucker. Look at me." The dog would not look but he sat up, his breath ragged and his tongue hanging, the rebar in his guts hanging out at an angle so as to touch the ground. Clayton prodded him with his boot again and said, "Move motherfucker," and this time the dog did move. Slowly, and as if with great effort, he turned around and tried to walk back into Old Man Solomon's yard. He took two steps then sat down again.

"Not so fast," Clayton said and then put himself between the dog and the yard. "Not so fast. Hey Danny—motor on back to my momma's and grab us a couple of beers from the fridge, will ya? It's hot as shit out here."

After Jenny and I had sparked, Jenny got up out of the closet and went and sat cross-legged with her back against her bed. I stayed in the closet on the piles of clothes that smelled like fresh laundry. She looked at me without speaking, looked through me without saying anything.

"What's up, Sis?" I asked.

"Nothing," she answered. "From here the closet looks so small."

I could still taste the Certs. It was on my teeth and mouth and in her breath and in the air.

"You ok?" I asked.

"With the light the way it is, I can hardly see you back there," she said.

I walked back over to Clayton's momma's and looked up at the sky. He was right; it was hot. It was that first really hot day of spring, summer before it's officially summer, and it felt like a record-breaker already and it was only early afternoon. Even the tree leaves were sweating. Spring would be over soon, and the green days done, until by August, the heat would turn everything into the color of a civil war photograph. Last August, I actually dreamt of water. I remembered the dream.

I got the beer from the fridge and by the time I walked them back to Clayton, little drops of condensation had formed on the cans, and the dog was back on its feet again.

Clayton cracked his beer and I cracked mine and he said, "Check it out. The little bastard won't give up!" and sure enough the dog was walking slowly and stiffly, like it was walking on glass. It tried to walk around Clayton into Old Man Solomon's yard but he moved a few feet to block it every time and slowly but surely edged it out to the sidewalk, away from the yard. *HAHAHAHA* it breathed now, loud enough I couldn't believe people couldn't hear it. Most of them were working; people like my momma, and kids were in their houses or at the mall or something. The dog walked and sat, walked and sat, and Clayton, with me alongside, herded it away from its yard.

"So what did you come over for in the first place?" Clayton asked me, as we maneuvered the dog along the sidewalk. The rebar hanging out its side dragged on the concrete and mad an ungodly sound, like fingernails on a chalkboard. "I'm sure it wasn't about this," he nodded at the dog and spat at it again.

"Um, yeah," I said, "it's about a girl. A girl I like. There's a dance next week and I want to ask her to dance but only if I know for sure she'll say yes."

Clayton laughed. "Ain't any way to guarantee that," he said. "Who is she?"

"Heidi Weller," I said, and I sighed.

"I know the family," he said, "She's a rich kid. She's got a lot of friends."

"I know."

By then, we had come to the edge of town: the edge of the trailer park really, and the road just ran out of town out past the landfill and out to little old farms like Old Man Solomon's before he sold and moved into town. Ain't any money in these little farms, save the real estate when it's sold to developers. Old Man Solomon got his money and in time, his old neighbors will get theirs.

We had the dog in the middle of the road and he lied down, breathing hard. His jaws were open impossibly wide, his tongue hung to the asphalt below, and his eyes were so wide there was more white than orange. Still, he wouldn't look at us. He turned his head if we walked up. Clayton tried to prod him along with his steel-toed boot again, but this time the dog did not move. He just panted and looked away.

There was a fence alongside the road and a tree with branches that overhung the fence. "Come on," Clayton said, "let's go sit on the fence under that tree and grab some shade. It's way too fucking hot out here today."

We went to sit in the shade and drank our beer. It was so hot out, the beer was already getting warm, and where the first swallows went down like *Manna* from heaven, the last few were a bit sour on the stomach.

"Well," said Clayton, drawing it out. "Here's how I'd do it. One: She's got a lot of friends, so ask a few of them to dance first. If they are friends with Heidi, they're not gonna be the fatties anyway. They're probably other cool kids—just not as cool as Heidi. This way, Heidi will see you're just out there having fun.

If you zero in on her, it'll set her radar off and she'll say no. No girl wants to be some guy's only option. Not at a middle school dance. It's loser-ish. Maybe even a bit stalker-ish. So work your way up."

I nodded and took another pull of warm beer.

"Secondly," he said, "don't be too polite. That'll set her radar off, too. After you let her see you out there with her friends, and you're just a guy having fun, go on up and say 'Let's go!' Don't ask her—tell her. Hold out your hand. She'll go. She might look at her friends and shrug her shoulders like she *has* to do this, but trust me, girls like to dance. She'll dance. And would you fucking look at that?"

The sun had moved behind the tree and the shade from its branches touched the road. The black dog had gotten up and staggered into the shade before lying down again, lying in the shade at that same awkward angle it had when first the rebar had stuck in its guts, the rebar pointing into the sky. The rebar was not so straight up now, more like at an angle. It wavered a little with each hard breath drawn.

Clayton set his empty can on a fence

post; I noticed the can was smeared a red color. It's from the condensation on the can, the sweat on his hands, and the rust from the rebar. He walked out to the dog and tried to get it to move with a few prods from his boot, but the dog wouldn't move. He grabbed the protruding end of the rebar and wiggled it a bit—that got the dog going. *HAHAHAHA* it breathed again with a half a snarl, his jaws wide open, and his eyes rolling wildly. He looked at Clayton, and I can't tell if it was fear or hate or begging for mercy, but Clayton got him back out to the middle of the road by steering him with the rebar, got him out of the shade and into the sun before he let him lie down again.

"Not on my watch," Clayton said as he came back and sat on the fence. "Now, after you have danced with her, tell her you want her to save one more. I'm sure she'll say sure or yes or whatever, but the key is, don't actually ask again. If she asks you, great—that's great. That's how it's supposed to work. But you never want to ask her again. Just don't. One step at a time and this is as good as it'll get for now."

The last of my beer, warm and sour, had gone down and I watched the dog half on its side, half on its back, wide mouthed in the sun.

God, it was hot. The sweat on my forehead ran down into my eyes even in the shade. I imagined Heidi now in a red summer dress, red and white with a red bandana on her wrist and still with a single long braid. I imagined her with her friends and I imagined them laughing. I did laugh a bit this time. Clayton was watching the dog and either didn't hear me or thought I was laughing at the dog.

"Have you ever asked a girl to dance this way, Clayton?" is all I can think to ask.

"Who? Me?" he laughed. "Not me, man. I let 'em come to me. I have abs. But if you gotta ask, you gotta come up with a different plan." He patted his stomach and it was hard and you could see the cuts and the blue vein that ran up from inside his jeans from his groin.

All I could do was nod. The dog was totally on its side now, the rebar pointed almost straight up again. I could see a fat red clot like a crimson leech on the pavement where it had come out of the wound. Flies were starting to come, but he was still breathing. I could hear it and see the ribcage moving, moving hard like he was running uphill. In the afternoon sun, the pavement had to feel like a lake of fire.

"Yeah, not so tough now," Clayton said, looking at the dog. "Say what Danny— why don't you run on back to Momma's and grab us two more beers. It's hotter than hell out here. I'll watch the damn dog. In a while, in a little while, I'll go pull the rebar out of the fucker. We'll leave him there like he's been run over. Kind of shits all over Old Man Solomon's bullshit about that dog never being out of the yard. That ol' bastard never even named it, you know that? Won't even miss it. No one will miss it. No one will miss Solomon when he's gone either. You know, at the end of the day, everyone, *everything* gets exactly what it deserves."

<hr />

"So you didn't smoke weed, you just sparked?"

I asked Jenny twice. She didn't hear me the first time. She was just looking into the closet. The sun the way it was, I was in shadow, in darkness, and I was sure she could hardly see me and those little specks of dust rising in the air like a screen, like smoke.

"No," she finally answered, "We did some other stuff."

It was my turn to be quiet now. I waited on her.

"We kissed," she said finally. "Clayton kissed me. We had sparked the last candy. We sat there just looking at each other and he asked if I wanted him to kiss me and I didn't say anything and he leaned forward and did it."

I said nothing.

"It's OK," she said, "It's OK, I wanted it to happen."

"Imma leave now," I said, and got up and got out of the closet. Jenny still sat there, cross-legged with her back against her little bed. All her stuffed animals were in a line up against her pillows.

I ran to get the beers from Clayton's momma's but walked 'em back. I didn't want them to foam up. Plus, it was too hot to run both ways. I thought again of Heidi Weller, I thought of her now in jeans and a sleeveless T-shirt like Jenny's jeans and Jenny's shirt. I thought of her in the closet and I thought of sparking with her. Her eyes were brown and in the darkness they caught just a bit of the last light of afternoon and they flashed like garnets and she puts the candy in her mouth. I can't see her hair but I know it's in a long braid hanging down her back. I wonder what it feels like, how soft it must be to touch. It's so hot; another beer would be a really good idea. Our momma wouldn't approve but I hardly think about that now. I get to the fence in the shade of the tree and hand Clayton his beer and we pop 'em both at the same time. The first swallow is so cold, so good. Clayton gestures towards the black dog with the can in his hand. "It won't be long now," he said.

HAHAHAHAHA its breath came again, only ragged and uneven, like a motor that won't start.

"You're a cool kid and all, Dan," Clayton said, his eyes still on the black dog. "But it's best you keep this between you and me. I mean, we'd be heroes to every kid in the park, but there is always some do-gooder that'll shit himself silly over a dog. So we don't say nothin' to nobody, *capisce?*"

I nodded my head and kept my eyes on the dog.

"You can tell Jenny, of course," he adds. "You guys are twins. I know how close twins are. She's a good kid, like you. She won't say anything."

I nodded again and took a long pull from my beer. So cold. So good. God, the heat.

King of Diamonds, King of Hearts

We don't come from much but we don't come from nothing either.

When we were young, we had this beat up deck of cards. All of the aces were gone, and some other cards too. We had maybe thirty-six cards out of a fifty-two-card deck. We'd play War, but we had to make up our own rules to account for the missing cards. "I've done the math" is how Danny put it, so in alternate games, the King of Hearts would be the highest card in the deck, then the King of Diamonds. No ties, no "wars" with those two cards. They were the highest cards we had, and they ruled, each in their turn, a diminished kingdom.

Dad left before I could remember. Danny said he could remember a bit. Mom worked two jobs most of the time, and we lived in a rent-subsidized townhouse with new neighbors every six months, and we walked to school, walked to get groceries, walked to catch a bus if we had to go anywhere else. Summers were slow, summers were hot.

One Saturday in June, after school let out for the summer and Mom didn't have to work, she sent us to get some groceries with a list and twenty dollars. That would leave enough change to get grape sodas out of the cooler there that opened from the top. You don't see that kind of cooler much any more. On the way back, walking slow and nursing my grape soda until it was warm, my plastic bag tore under the weight of its contents and a package of hamburger fell out, fell in terrible slow-motion and hit the sidewalk with a soft wet slap. The cellophane tore and the hamburger laid half on its Styrofoam bed and half on the sidewalk and I could see little specks of dirt and gravel on the meat and the blood of it left a ring on the concrete.

"Shit," Danny said.

I said nothing, but two tears, hot on my face even with the sweat of a hot June day on it, rolled on down to fall and join the bloodstain on the sidewalk.

"Take my bags," Danny said, and looked around to see if anyone saw us. No one had, or no one cared, and I took his bags and he took the hamburger, laid it gently with his hands back on the Styrofoam bed and picked up all the cellophane wrapping, too, and started walking. "We'll wash it at the park," he said, and I really had to hustle to keep up.

There was a drinking fountain at the park and Danny very carefully rinsed the hamburger, picking the bigger bits of gravel out of it with his fingers. When he was satisfied it was clean, he even more carefully massaged it back on the Styrofoam bed and wrapped the cellophane over it as tightly as he could, repositioning it so as to place the tear at the bottom of the package, underneath the Styrofoam. Flies were starting to find us and I shooed them away, this was as much help as I was. Two kids came up and wanted to use the fountain and just stood there while Danny was washing the meat. "What are you doing?" they asked in unison.

"Fuck off already," was Danny's answer, without looking up.

When he was satisfied that he was finished, we drank the last of our grape sodas and refilled the bottles with water from the fountain and we walked home and turned over the groceries to mom. We had spaghetti with meat sauce that night. Red and warm.

On Monday, we were mostly alone because Mom worked. We played in the park all day and went home at six for supper. When we walked in, there was this man sitting at the kitchen table. A short man, with thick shoulders and hands, wearing brown overalls, a pork-pie hat and a white v-neck T-shirt under the overalls. He smiled under a graying goatee.

"Who are you?" I asked. Danny said nothing.

"Patrick, Daniel. I'm your old man," he said, and smiled bigger. He got up from the table and hugged me and he smelled like sweat and a cigarette and WD-40. Danny didn't hug him; he stuck his hand straight out and they shook hands. The guy still smiled. "I remember you," was all Danny said.

We ate leftover spaghetti, and Mom suggested things to ask him, but I just sat there and stared at him. Danny had nothing to ask him either. Mom had her hair down. I never saw her hair down; she normally wore it up. I couldn't think of him as "my old man." I thought of him as "the guy." But if Mom brought it up a question for us to ask we didn't have to ask because then he'd answer her directly. It was like they were talking about him, to him.

The next day, he took Danny to work with him so I was on my own at the park. The afternoon was hot and I mostly stayed in the house playing games of "War" with myself with the deck and the Red Kings, careful to remember who was high card in each game and alternating them as per Danny's math. Apparently our father was a handyman of some sort and he had a job working for a big landlord, swapping out air-conditioning units in the apartments the landlord owned. Every apartment had one of those little units that fit in a window and they were all getting new ones. On Danny's first day on the job they came back with an old unit and put it in our kitchen window. "Shhh—don't tell anyone," the old man said with a wink and he and Danny hooked it up. Danny now called him "The Old Man" and so I did, too. Mom folded her arms across her chest and had a look about her I couldn't quite figure out but she watched them put it in and it worked and the kitchen was a whole lot cooler and the rest of our place a little cooler, too.

This went on until Friday when the old

man dropped Danny off for supper and went somewhere on his own. We ate supper in our cool kitchen and played cards and went to bed early—Danny was tired from working and I had nothing to do. It was hot, even with the new air-conditioner, and I tossed and turned and dreamt fragments of dreams. I would close my eyes and drop the hamburger again and again, drop it with that wet slap and the flies would come and I'd drop it again and hear my mother cry and Danny was yelling, yelling at me and I'd drop it again and my hands were heavy and my head so hot and I could not for the life of me pick it up except to drop it and I wanted to run away but I could not, I was rooted to the spot. I woke up.

I got out of bed and in the hallway between our rooms, the Old Man was hitting Mom, hitting her with a half a fist: his nails in the palm of his hand, his thumb not quite closed and hitting her in the side of the head and her hair would shake. Her hair was down and her hands were over her face and he'd hit her on the ear and her hair would bounce and she'd cover up more and that was the sound, the sound in my dream of the hamburger hitting the pavement and my mother crying.

Danny was yelling and he ran up to the Old Man, his head under the Old Man's chin and his palms on the Old Man's chest and he drove him up and back, up and back, and the Old Man reached up for balance and then fell back over, fell back down the stairs, ass-over-tea-kettle, ridiculous in his brown overalls and sweaty white T-shirt smelling like a thousand cigarettes. When he went over, I could see his calves naked above his socks and he went over twice like that with his hands on his head to protect it and came to a stop on his ass, facing the other way at the bottom of the stairs. The neighbors on either side were banging the walls with their fists and with broom handles, banging, banging, banging and shouting muffled shouts but when the Old Man fell and Mom quit crying and Danny quit shouting they stopped.

"Danny, Danny, Danny!" my mom said, her hands still on her face, "No! No! No! Someone will come!"

Danny stood at the top of the stairs breathing hard, red-faced, fist clenched tightly, but very quiet, and the Old Man sat at the bottom with his back towards us. Without looking up, he patted himself down, making a show of it to let us see that he was all right, letting us wonder what was going to happen next. He got up and sat on the bench by the front door and put on his workman's boots without tying up the laces. He stood up without looking at any of us, put on his pork-pie hat and shuffled out the door, shutting it quietly behind him. We heard the soles of his boots scuff across the walk until he got into his truck and started it. Then he was gone. We never saw the Old Man ever again.

"Ain't no one coming," Danny said finally, "No one." Then he hit the wall, the wall where the heat of previous summers had warped the paint and the belongings of previous tenants had scored it with gouges only half filled in. He hit it a few times with his fists and shouted "Fuck off already!" after each blow and no banging came from the neighbors in reply.

"Patrick," he said to me "It's OK. You can stop crying. He's gone."

I guess I was crying.

When Danny graduated, he went into the service and went to Afghanistan. When I graduated and eventually got into university, he came back.

I asked him "What about Afghanistan?" and all he said was "It smells like weed, sweat, and shit." And that was about it.

"Did you shoot anyone?"

"Nah," he said. "Spec Forces got 'em all. We just walked around a lot. It was hot. Army life. Lots of 'hurry up and wait.'" And that was that.

He put on a lot of muscle in the service. He got tatted up, too—a full sleeve on his left arm. Bands he liked. Phrases he loved. "Crooked Saints, Stand-Up Villains" one said. On his right shoulder, he got a King of Diamonds and a King of Hearts. He asked me if I knew where he got the idea for that one.

"I remember," I told him. "You know, Mom had those cards out at a garage sale last year. No one would buy them because it wasn't a full deck—but all the little kids too young to read wanted them. I kept 'em. Got 'em in my room." He liked that.

He got a job bouncing at a strip club. He joked that it was a high school reunion every weekend—on both sides of the stage. "Times are tough," he told me, "but the Titty Trade survives." He'd make five hundred some nights hustling tables.

These guys would come in: bankers or finance people, guys in suits, and the place would be dead, but he'd stop them at the door and apologize and tell them that he had a reservation coming in an hour, so the best tables—up front on "Gynecology Row"—were reserved. Their group would have to sit in the back. The suits were like "What the fuck—they're empty now," and he'd look around and say "Well ok—I can do you a favor and sit you up there now, but when my party comes in you gotta move," and they'd be happy. The place would fill up in an hour or so and sure enough, a new group of guys would come in and start looking around and he'd tell them "In the back—you gotta sit in the back— that's all we got room for," and the new group would not be happy, and he'd say "I'll tell ya what—those guys up there?" and he'd point to the guys on Gynecology Row, "I can probably move 'em and put you in that table but it's gonna cost something." The new group would pony up—often a hundred bucks but never less than fifty. Danny would take the money, walk on up to the first group and tell 'em his reservation had arrived—they had to move. And they would.

He'd hustle tables like that all night.

Once in a while, one of the guys he served with would come in, and when Danny was off they'd sit and have a few drinks, watch the girls, and listen to whatever the DJ had on. I went and sat with him once, on a Tuesday if you can believe it. Some suits in there had figured out they were vets and were sending shots over to Danny and his buddy who would always thank them but mostly stuck to their beer. They'd pass the shots on to the girls.

Danny got up to go to the bathroom and when he was gone the guy leaned in and asked me "How does Danny sleep?"

"Good, as far as I know," I answered. Which was true. He had his own place now. Air-conditioned, if that matters.

"What did he tell you about Afghanistan?"

"Not much. Said it smelled like weed, sweat, and shit, and that he never even fired a shot in anger."

"Well that's true, I guess," the guy said, watching the bathroom door to see if Danny was coming. "Did he tell you he killed a guy with a shovel?"

"He did not," is all I could say, and my beer tasted warm.

"Yeah. Fuck. Killed this kid with a shovel. Fucking *haji* trying to set up a mine. Spotters had seen something suspicious, so we went on patrol, walking the road. Hajis like to plant their improvised explosive devices on the road to take out the gas tankers going to Kabul. It's a big win for them if they can do that. Makes life hard in Kabul and if you've ever seen a tank full of octane explode you know it's a hell of a show. It looks good on their videos. It was July, in a place where you could see Kashmir in the distance, the moon still visible even during the day. Shangri La. It's so beautiful, it's distracting. It's Africa-hot out there; fat-kid-killing hot. You've been told about the smell. We're in forty pounds of gear, just wet with sweat. I swear you don't get that wet swimming. We have an armored fighting vehicle called a Stryker backing us up and at one point the commander thought he'd seen movement in this field so he put about a hundred rounds from the fifty into the field and we went in on foot. Danny's got a shovel off of the Stryker. Sometimes—all the time actually—the fucking hajis would just throw some dirt over the improvised explosives if they thought they'd been seen, so they don't have anything on them when we catch them. Rules of Engagement says we gotta let 'em go if they are empty-handed. They'll come back later and set it up. But we want to find the bomb so they can't come back and set it up. Plus, rumor had it the hajis had bought some special ones, some of what they call explosively formed projectiles from Iranian connections and those cock-biters can take out a main battle tank. So here we are, in the heat, walking through rows of marijuana plants—"

"—Weed?" I interrupted

"You know it, bro. Remember what your brother told you about the smell? Weed and opium are the only things those poor bastards can grow for cash over there. They have a metric ass-load of it. Plus, it's not forbidden in the Koran. Anyway, they cultivate it in long rows and they flood-irrigate so between each row is a little ditch, more often than not fertilized with human shit. There's the smell again. It's fucking disgusting. So we're walking along, row by row, shit by shit, and I have my rifle at my shoulder and Danny's got a shovel and we're in past the point where we can see the Stryker up on the road when Danny practically steps on the guy. The haji had hidden down there in the rows in his long brown shirt and pants and just hoped we wouldn't find him, but we did and he got up and tried to run still holding a plastic bag filled with explosives. Danny's after him and I'm yelling 'Down, down, down!' because I know I can shoot the fucker but I'm afraid I'll hit Danny. But Danny—your bro is an athlete by the way—caught the guy by the collar and slung him back around on the ground and then as they say, a fight broke out. Somehow, Danny gets a knee on the guy's chest like he's schoolyarding him. Our guys are starting to shoot down their rows. Everyone's yelling 'Contact! Contact! Contact!' and sending rounds down their rows but it's really just Danny and the haji. These fucking hajis are never more than fifteen years old and might weigh a buck-twenty-five if they've eaten that day. The haji is—I can't quite describe it—he's clawing at Danny, his hands like he's treading water or climbing a ladder and Danny's got a knee on his chest and he's stabbing at the kids hands with the shovel yelling 'Stop! Stop! Stop!' but the guy doesn't and Danny starts stabbing at him with the shovel a lot harder now—adrenaline and all—and pretty soon, he's just fucking hacking the guy apart. CHUNK! CHUNK! CHUNK! The shovel is hitting bone, and I can remember this part very clearly:

at one point, he hacks him so hard with the shovel, he cuts off one of the guy's fingers, and the thing cartwheels in the air like a fat red fly almost above Danny before coming down and finally CHUNK! and the guy dies with Danny on his chest and the last bit of air rattles out of him like a slashed tire, and he has almost no face left. Already, there are flies on him, flies and dirt. That fine brown dirt that's like silt is filling in his face. Already. I put my hand on Danny's shoulder to get him off the guy and he threw up, thin and sour, on my boots and on the ground and there's a lot of that in Afghanistan, too."

I said nothing.

"Hey bro, it's not like it's a crime," he said. "I'm not sure the Rules of Engagement would have been an issue man, but when we debriefed, we told the Lieutenant that we found the guy that way. We said that we thought he'd taken a round from the fifty on the Stryker when the Stryker commander hosed the field. The bag had a bunch of Semtex from the Russian days—more than enough to set off a tanker, and some other shit. Bomb-making shit. We gave it to the engineers. I don't know what they did with it. They are supposed to blow it up but Afghanistan has way more of that shit than we have engineers, so for all I know someone still has it. Anyway, officially the guy took a round from the fifty on the Stryker. But you can bet your ass I made sure word got out around base, and your brother should have gotten a Purple Heart for being injured by high-five. Everyone hates the fucking roadside bombs. Everyone loves your brother. Those bombs, those IEDs, are a chickenshit way to wage war. Killing a guy with a shovel—that's straight up honorable. Straight up."

Danny came back from the bathroom in good spirits, jerked his thumb towards the booth and said he'd gotten the DJ to throw some Guns N' Roses on. "G N-fucking R, man," he said, and then "What have you ladies been up to?"

"Talking about Afghanistan and how you say it smells like weed, sweat, and shit," his buddy told him.

"That it does," Danny said in return, "That it does."

The guys who had been buying us shots sent over another round and "Paradise City" came on and we toasted each other and hammered a shot and sang with the G N-fucking R.

We decided to finish all the shots those guys sent us, and the rest of the night I don't remember all that much of, but I woke up the next morning just in time to not pee the bed. When I was in the John, I looked in the mirror and saw I had a new tattoo: a King of Diamonds and a King of Hearts.

A couple of years and a couple of binges later, we got some scrollwork done below the two Kings. "I have done the math," it said. I just had to look at it and I'd laugh. It was a moment in time. You had to be there. No girlfriend I have ever understands.

Danny left the club. He had some trouble, beat up a few guys, typical strip-club bouncer shit. There were charges, some of them dropped, some got plead down. A couple of lawsuits.

"One too many assholes," the club owner said. "It all adds up."

He was referring to the people who walked in through the front door. He understood how it could be, working the door at a place like that, but it was best if Danny moved on. You can't beat up everyone just because they need it.

Danny talked about re-enlisting, but he opened a gym instead. Mixed-martial arts stuff. He was always the baddest guy in there. Guys wanted to train with him, wanted his tattoos, wanted his reputation. I graduated from university. I wasn't all that bad—but I had the tattoos. The gym was downtown on a one-way street. Danny had a beater of a pick-up he used to run errands for the gym and on Saturdays when the traffic was lighter, he'd park right in front—right across two angled, metered stalls, load/unload because he could do it faster than if he had to park a block away.

Saturday in August, nine in the morning and no one around, and Danny and I are unloading flats of Gatorade and carrying it in the gym. There weren't many flats so he let the truck idle and left the radio on and we unloaded to whatever songs came on. After the last flat had been put away, we came back out and he's getting ticketed. The parking enforcement officer, some old guy in a little uniform, was there writing Danny up.

"Are you shitting me?" Danny said to the guy, "It's Saturday!"

The guy wouldn't answer.

"Are you fucking shitting me? There's no one else here!" Danny said again, walking up behind the guy, walking within arm's reach.

The guy wouldn't answer, just walked away.

"Are you going to fucking answer me?" Danny asked, quieter now, and I was too far away to do anything. The guy just walked faster.

Danny put an arm around the guy and slung him to the ground, spinning him around and choking him hard. The old guy wheezed and his eyes got wide. I ran up to them, trying to get Danny to look me in the eye.

"Danny," I said, my hand on his shoulder, "Let the guy go. He's only doing his job. I'll pay the fucking ticket. I'll pay it in pennies. Fuck the city. Just let go." But Danny just choked him harder. The guy wheezed, a thin and high and lonely sound, a sigh. Tears rolled down his cheeks and he blew bubbles out his nose. His hands fluttered along Danny's arms and back towards his face but Danny kept his chin down and held on. I had my hands on Danny's forearm, trying to get my fingers in between Danny and the guy's throat but I just couldn't; Danny, all muscle and ink and rage, was just too strong.

"Tell me when you smell shit!" Danny said and really bore down on the guy and held him for the length of a song, the music coming from Danny's truck. The guy's eyes closed and I smelled shit and he was dead, his lips covered in spit and snot and his pants full of his own bodily wastes and he was dead in Danny's arms, his little meter guy's hat out in the middle of the street. Dead.

"You gotta go," I said to Danny, standing there, but Danny held the guy—hard like he had been, for the length of another song. When the song ended and advertisements began to play he let the guy flop over and then stood up and dragged him to the curb and propped him up in a sitting position and just looked at him. The smell of feces was overwhelming and flies had begun to come around. There was a wet spot on Danny's T-shirt where the guy's head had been against Danny's chest; whether from Danny's sweat or the dead guy's, I do not know. Both, I think.

"Danny, you gotta go."

"No," he said. "Someone will come."

"No Dan, just get on out. I'll call an ambulance. I'll say I just found him here."

"Nah," he said, and sat down beside the guy, brushing the flies away. "Where's your cell phone?"

"In the truck," I said and motioned with my head.

"Go on and call an ambulance."

"I think he's dead."

"Well. Maybe they can bring him back. That might be good. Can you just call someone? Anyone?"

Danny had an arm around the guy now, to keep him upright, and was still shooing the flies away. The smell was intolerable. I went and got the phone and walked back over.

"Do you remember that week the Old Man came back when we were kids?" Danny asked me.

"Yeah," I said. "It wasn't that long ago, really."

"You know that week I worked with him, swapping out those air-conditioners in those apartments?"

"Yep."

"You know he never paid me right? Nothing. I know we gave him the boot before the job was over but still, he should have paid me. He said he'd pay me."

I nodded.

"What he was doing was taking the new air-conditioners and selling them out of the truck to acquaintances for quick cash. He'd take the cash and buy old air-conditioners—way older than the ones we were pulling out—and put those in. He would pocket the difference. If anyone asked, he'd say they were 'refurbished' and as good as new. 'Full warranty,' he'd say, and whatever blah-blah-blah it took. The Old Man could talk. No one ever called him on it. The used ones he pulled out? He'd sell those too. It was one of those he put in our place. I think Mom knew something was up but she didn't know exactly. Anyway, he never paid me."

I nodded again.

Danny let the body down, gently, and laid it against the pavement. Flies started to settle on it, darting this way and that.

"Do you still have that deck of cards?" he asked. He never took his eyes off of the body. "The King of Diamonds, the King of Hearts? That deck?"

"I do," I told him, but I lied. Somewhere, in one of my moves, it had been lost.

"Is anyone coming?" he asked, less to me than to himself, still looking at the body.

"Someone will be here soon," I said. I walked back to Danny's truck. I turned the key in the ignition to shut it off and started to dial.

The Burning Pile

Two cousins of the same first and last names but different middle initials farmed on opposite sides of town. "John J." went by that name or, as a nickname, "One-Arm Johnny," on account of he had lost the use of one arm after an accident involving a grain augur. He wore long sleeves as a matter of course and a vest and tucked the remains of his arm in the pocket of the vest when he was out and about. He did things all right for a man with one arm.

John R., his cousin, a taller and leaner man, went by "John R" or "Too Tall Johnny" on account of his height, although in truth he wasn't that tall. He was cowboy-thin and taciturn. One-Arm Johnny was the talker of the two. Too-Tall Johnny smoked and didn't say much.

John R. had a dog, a big bouncy thing, long legged and blond, with lots of German

Shepherd in it and maybe some retriever or maybe some Red Heeler.

One April afternoon, Too Tall Johnny's neighbor a section away called him up.

"John R.," he said, "Nothing but bad news. Your dog has come and killed one of my lambs. You can see the tracks in the snow. You can come see it for yourself."

Too-Tall Johnny said he'd be right over and hung up. He grabbed his checkbook and his .22 long and got into his pickup. The inside of the truck smelled like cigarettes and wet straw, like every farm truck. The dog was in the yard, bouncing around like a big happy kid and jumped into the bed of the truck. Going for a ride. Dogs love to ride, smelling what comes by, nose in the air.

Johnny and the dog got over to the neighbor's in good time and met the man at the fence line. There in the snow was a dead lamb, and the dog's tracks leading back to Johnny's farmyard only a half a mile or so away. Johnny shook hands with his neighbor and apologized, then got out the checkbook and wrote the man a check for what he asked for. There was no argument.

When he was done, he grabbed the dog out of the back of the truck, grabbed it with both hands by the scruff of the neck and slung it to the ground, right on top of the murdered lamb. The dog cowered and looked one way, then the other, and its tail flicked low over the snow. It had light brown eyes, that odd color that appears only in some dogs. Almost orange. The man held the dog so tightly by the face it had to look him in the eye, but even so it tried to look away. It dug its front paws in, trying to pull away, but Too-Tall Johnny held it there a minute, held it firm.

"Don't ever do that again," Johnny said, his voice low. "Don't ever do that again or I'm going to have to shoot you." His voice was deep. He made the dog look at him. For a moment, only a moment, its tail quit moving. It just sat on its haunches, its face in his hands. What does a dog know? Really know? Then its tail moved again and Too-Tall got up and apologized to the man once more and they shook hands again and he fired up the truck. The dog jumped in the back, a little less energetically than it had at first, and they were off home. The neighbor stood there with the check in his hand and his dead lamb on the ground and watched them drive off.

It kept snowing on and off for a couple more days. Not heavy, but enough to fill in the dog's tracks, if not the truck's. A little more sun came every day, it got a little warmer, but it was one of those years when spring was slow to come and the melt was held in abeyance.

The neighbor called. "John R.," he said, "I hate to tell you this, but your dog has been at my lambs again and killed another one. Same as last time. You can come and see for yourself. I'm sorry, John R., sorry to say it, but it's true."

John R. thanked him and hung up. He wrote a check out at the kitchen table then walked out to the truck. The dog was back, soft with its winter coat, a dirty but lively brown and gold against the new snow and his eyes were the color of cinnamon. It was in the bed of the truck before Too-Tall Johnny had it started. They drove to the neighbor's, the cab of the truck smelling like cigarettes and mud, the dog in the bed running from one side to the other to lean out past the cab and catch what smells came on down in the cold April air.

They got to the neighbor's and there, against the fence line in almost the same place as before was the man, a dead lamb, and tracks in the snow leading back to Too-Tall's farm. He apologized to the neighbor before the man could say anything and gave him the check, noting that he assumed it was the same for this one as for the other. The man nodded. Too-Tall got his .22 long out and pulled the bolt to chamber a round. With one hand, he grabbed the dog by the scruff of the neck and slung him out of the truck to the ground, slung him hard into the soft snow. The dog struggled and yelped but Too-Tall Johnny stood on it, one foot on its shoulder, and pinned it there until it submitted. It looked here and there and around and about but never at Johnny and its tail flicked up at uneven intervals, posing some sort of question. What do dogs ask? Too-Tall put the barrel of the .22 in the dog's ear and pulled the trigger. There was the soft "pop" of the .22 and the dog thrashed wildly for a second. Johnny lifted his foot and the dog's back legs came up and found some sort of purchase, and it snowplowed forward a foot or two, head dead but legs alive, halfway under the lowest strand of barbed wire on the fence a little past the dead lamb before it faltered and stopped. There was almost no blood, just a spat on the white snow. It might have come from the lamb.

Johnny put the gun back in the truck, picked up the dog with one hand on the scruff of its neck and the other on its tail and bucked it up into the truck bed. He walked around to his side, nodded at his neighbor and once again drove home while the man stood by his dead lamb with his check in his hand.

When Johnny got home, he backed up to the burning pile. Most farmers keep a burning pile for garbage they can't or don't want to take to the landfill. He dropped the tailgate, reached in and grabbed the dog by the tail and slid it one-handed onto the top of the pile. In a few days—a week-and-a-half at most—it would be warm enough to light it up, burn everything there. When the time came, when the wind warmed the air and dried the pile, he'd throw on some gas and a match and let it burn. He did that a couple of times a year, as need be. Same as everyone.

In the meantime, the dog would stiffen in the cold, on top of some shingles, moldy hay, splintered 2x4s, cardboard, plywood, a couple of dead calves, a hundred hard tumbleweeds, the dried stalks of things growing up from the bottom, potatoes from the garden pulled up too late in the fall, and a thousand spider webs too tough to disappear in winter.

The neighbor ran into One-Arm Johnny the next day out in front of the co-op, told him the whole story starting with the first lamb and Too Tall's conversation with his dog. One-Arm shrugged.

"That sounds like something John R. would do," he said, and walked on in.

Indolence and Rhyme

I decided that it was not wisdom that enabled poets to write their poetry, but a kind of instinct or inspiration, such as you find in seers and prophets who deliver all their sublime messages without knowing in the least what they mean.

-Socrates

Tania spent the first four hours of every Saturday caring for a mentally handicapped adult man named Shiloh.

"Shiloh?" She asked the program co-coordinator when she and Shiloh were introduced. "For real?"

"Shiloh," the woman said. Her name was Gretchen and she had some problems herself. Gretchen looked at Tania and said "Don't talk about him like he's not here. There is a person inside there, just like you and I."

"Terkle," Shiloh said.

They settled into a routine quickly enough. Tania would walk him around the bike path down by the river. She'd ask him "How did your parents come to name you 'Shiloh,' Shiloh?"

And he'd say "Terkle," and point at the river.

They'd walk a little farther.

"So you are saying you named yourself? After an imaginary friend you had when you were nine? That's actually pretty cool!" she'd say. Shiloh would laugh a half a laugh, like the last person in a room to get a joke but the one who enjoyed it the most. His laugh was the essence of his humanity, "Terkle" the essence of his "otherness."

So four hours would pass, at eleven-dollars per, and she'd be forty-four closer to making the rent and feeding the cats. That's what "Respite Worker" pays. She worked Mondays to Fridays at a call center. Mondays always started with an admonition to "up sell" and Fridays ended with people calling in sick in the morning and then other people quitting and walking out at noon. "I don't need this shit," they'd say, and they'd be gone and Tania and whoever was left that needed to make rent or feed the cats, would hang on.

Tania needed "the shit." A thousand bucks a month base and then another six-hundred to seven-hundred in commission and she needed that shit. At least Shiloh was easy going, as far as mentally handicapped adults go. He never soiled himself. "Terkle," and a wave of his hand and that was that.

Forty-four dollars. But that was before taxes and withholdings.

After she took him back to the home, she'd wait at the bus stop for the 1 p.m. to go home and feed her cats and smoke a fucking bowl with the TV on and the sound off. After a week in a headset Tania didn't need to hear human voices. They would just disturb the equilibrium the bowl brought her. She'd fall asleep on the couch and dream sinsemilla dreams until Monday when she would have to get up and shower and go back to the call center and try to get peoples' credit card numbers from them without being too-too clear about what the limitations were on the warranty they were buying. "You sell what's good for the house," her manager hissed at her once. The manager needed this shit, too.

There was a card and gift shop next to the bus stop; if any creepy homeless fucks were in the stop, she'd go into the card shop and idle around. Some of the cards were funny. A man sleeping in his own urine in a bus stop is not funny. In one section of the shop was a collection of journals, leather or fabric bound things with little brass clasps. Blue and black and red and brown. Some were blank, some had "My Journal" on them in embossed lettering.

Tania remembered when she used to write poetry, when she'd first started smoking, and she felt good all the time and always wrote high and was sure she was going to be something other than a call center captive and wheelchair jockey. She and her friend Shellie would write poetry in their journals and read to each other and buy those "streak and style" kits from the discount pharmacy (or shoplift them when they didn't have any money) and color each other's hair with reds and greens.

Shellie's poetry was good; it always

rhymed. Sometimes Tania could not get hers to rhyme. One time they had smoked a little too much weed maybe, or written a little too much poetry longing for this boy or that or whatever and Shellie had written something nice about her. Tania could not remember the poem at all, but she did remember that they had made out a bit after Shellie read it to her and stopped after they had French-kissed and Tania didn't know if she liked it or not. She opened up the journal to the frontispiece and read:

"Forever is Composed of Nows"

-Emily Dickenson

What if your nows all suck? she thought. My nows all suck. That's why they feel like forever. She wished she could afford to smoke a bowl Saturday *and* Sunday. But "that's how rich people live, not us," she'd once told her cats, when thinking it out loud. Occasionally she allowed herself a bowl Thursday because Fridays at the call center were the sucky now, squared. She wished that Shiloh had a prescription worth stealing but apparently he had nothing. "He's off his meds," was never a phrase uttered in regards to Shiloh.

She took a pen out from her purse, looked around to see if anyone was watching, then wrote *Go fuck yourself Emily* under the quote and put the journal back.

She noted the price tag—$18.99—a little less than half of what she'd net pushing Shiloh around after taxes, so she took the journal back out and wrote *Yea, go fuck yourself, verily* under her first phrase.

The rhyme made her happy and she was pleased that her printing was still neat. I don't print like a stoner with three cats and no life, she thought.

She opened it again and wrote another line yet, to make it read:

> *Go fuck yourself Emily*
> *Yea, go fuck yourself, verily,*
> *You and your fucking nows*

She put the journal back quickly then left the store and waited for the bus stop. $18.99 for a journal? She could pack a bowl for less, and she needed the bowl more. Speaking of which, time to go home and pack that bowl. This was going to be a good one. She could feel it.

The next Saturday, she picked up Shiloh. "Hey Shiloh! Wanna go Terkle-ing?" she asked. He laughed his delayed-reaction laugh, pure and simple, and seemed really happy. Truthfully, she thought, he's not hard to like, in his own weird way. Gretchen watched them walk out, and waved. Tania noticed that Gretchen had no hand, just a stump. Strange how I had not noticed that before, she thought. Maybe she'd had an prosthesis on. One of those plastic and metal contraptions. I wonder what happened?

When she brought Shiloh back, she stopped to talk to Gretchen. "How much does this pay?" she asked, meaning Gretchen's job.

"To be honest, not much," Gretchen said. "In fact, it's a subsidized position anyway. I live from grant to grant. If they—the organization— don't get the grant, I'm unemployed. In fact, it's grant application time now. If I'm not here in a month, you know what happened."

"Did you always want to do this?" Tania asked.

"*No*," said Gretchen. "Never even thought about it. I'm an introvert. I wanted to be a writer. A poet actually. How silly is that? I have a ton of little journals at home filled with my writing. No one has ever seen them. Then *this* happened," She held up her stump.

"How did *that* happen?" Tania asked.

"Meh. It's a long story," Gretchen said, looking away. "Let's just say it was electrical and leave it at that."

"Electrical?"

"Yes. Electrical. The thing is, I wrote everything in longhand. And I'm right handed. Now with no right hand..." she sighed audibly, "I can't write anything more than my name left-handed. Occupational therapy tried to teach me but that was it. Don't even suggest typing. Typing is for data entry. You can't type poetry. Maybe some can, but I can't. It wouldn't be right. For me anyway. Well, at some point in the process I told the rehab people I was a poet and they thought about it and found me this job. A grant came in and here I am."

Tania nodded. She noticed that Gretchen had a lazy eye, too. She wondered if that was "electrical."

"You know, I like you Tania. That's why

I gave you Shiloh. He's our star. Never shits his pants. Never grabs a boob."

Shiloh wasn't within earshot so it was all right to talk about him as if he wasn't there.

She left Gretchen and her electrified stump and lazy eye and went over to the gift shop and straight to the pink fabric covered journal. She'd had one just like it when she and Shellie had kissed. The girl at the counter was texting on her cell phone and didn't acknowledge Tania when she came in. The "Emily Dickenson" journal was still there. Tania smiled at that. She checked again and sure that she would not be seen, opened the fabric journal near the middle. With her pen, she printed *You will read this* and then:

> *You have twelve years*
> *Nine months*
> *And three days*
> *Before you die*
> *Use it well*
> *Or not at all*
> *It's up to you*
> *There is nothing else you can do*
> *Try not to dwell on this*

The thought of someone finding that after filling the previous pages with hearts and their "married" name when thinking of their crush really pleased her. She had an opinion of who bought fabric covered journals and of what went into them: rhymes about sadness never personally experienced, and ballpoint pen drawings of hearts and flowers and surnames from boys who would never talk to the writer because they were stupid and never knew what they were supposed to do. Her printing was neater than ever. Thank God she still had her right hand, she thought. At least I have that.

It did not rhyme, but Tania had never been good at rhyming. She thought of Shellie and wondered if Shellie would be able to make it rhyme. They had lost touch but she did not wish to find her. What for? To talk about that one time they kissed and how they used to write poetry together but now no one could make ends meet even on two jobs and they all had roomfuls of cats and no one wrote anymore?

On the way out, the girl at the counter looked up at Tania. She was quite fat and spoke very nasally. "If you are thinking about buying one of the journals, wait a week or two. It's not official but the owner is shutting this place down. No one buys anything anymore. Those journals are $18.99 now but they'll be half that in a month."

"Thanks," Tania said, and then, "I'll be back. For sure."

She walked out to the 1 p.m. Once she was home, she smoked her fucking bowl and it was even better than the last one. She dreamt that she had no hands and was naked in a shopping mall. No one looked at her. She didn't care. She was weightless, ascendant, and no one spoiled it by looking. Then Shellie came into the dream, Shellie, only one hundred pounds heavier than she had been when they wrote poetry together all those times and even kissed. Shellie told her to "get her shit tighter," and all of a sudden Tania was dressed but still had no hands. "Get your shit together doesn't rhyme, Shellie," she said, and Shellie asked, "What are you talking about?" Shellie's belly poked out from under her shirt and over her jeans. She was leading a small boy by the hand and Tania said "Shiloh?" and the boy said "Terkle" and laughed and Shellie yanked on his arm and led him away from Tania. Tania, heavy-legged and slow with the weight of sleep again, unascendant, could not keep up.

Tania woke up and wasn't even mad. That was some excellent weed, she thought. The cats looked happy, too. They can feel your mood but not dream your dreams. They dream of cat things. Murder, copulation, sleep—if it is possible to dream of sleep, cats would dream of it. She could not be sure how a little second-hand marijuana smoke affected them, but they never complained.

Monday came and she started thinking about doing a Thursday bowl by 10 a.m.

Saturday came and she picked up Shiloh for their terkle-walk. Gretchen was with him.

"Guess what?" Gretchen said. She had her prosthetic on. It looked good, almost like a real hand. The nails were painted red, as though she had just had a manicure.

"What?" Tania asked.

"Less grant money this year. This is the last time you'll see me. Technically I'm here to month-end but I have a bunch of unused holiday time they want me to take so I will take it and use the time to look for another job."

"That's terrible!" said Tania. Gretchen's electrically bad eye looked up and away, perhaps at her uncertain future. Or maybe a terkle. Who knows?

"No worries," said Gretchen, "I'll get something else. Maybe some call center work; they're always hiring. I can handle a headset and I can work the phone keys easily. Especially if they have touch-screens. Ever work on a touch-screen computer? They're awesome. As long as I don't have to write anything, I'll be OK, and believe it or not I still qualify for some disability. Who knows, I could be back here and you could be looking after me! Hey, Shiloh, wouldn't that be something? We could all walk along the river and look for turtles."

"Terkles!" Shiloh said, quite loudly. It was the happiest Tania had ever seen him

"Turtles?" Tania asked.

"Yeah—turtles," Gretchen said. Her bad eye had come around; she looked almost normal. "He likes turtles. He calls them 'terkles' because he thinks it's funny. Either that or they were called 'terkles' back where he was from originally. He's a bit of a hillbilly. I told you there is a person in there. You're a bit of a joker, aren't you Shiloh?"

She reached over and mock-punched him in the shoulder.

He laughed his easy laugh, quicker than usual, and longer. He beamed.

Gretchen kept on, "He thinks turtles live in the river. They don't. Not in these parts. Too cold. Maybe they did back where he was from. But he's pretty sure that one day, he'll find one. I'm surprised he hasn't told you. But he can be shy."

Tania looked at Shiloh. He would not look back. He just smiled and waited.

"At any rate, you two look after each other."

Tania took Shiloh out along the river. No turtles appeared.

After she returned him, she went back to the card shop.

"One more week," the counter girl said. "Then everything is on sale."

Tania went to the journals. She picked a handsome one, red leather with metal at the corners and a little clasp. She opened it and smelled the paper. Paper always smells good. The better the paper and the older it is the better it smells. This journal in particular smelled really good. She watched the counter girl until she was sure the girl was engrossed in her phone again, then took out her pen, and on the very last page of the journal wrote:

When I was young
If you had asked me
I would have said that all
I wanted to do was write poetry
I wanted to be a poet more than anything
Now I work in a call center
And look after a "cognitively impaired" man
I have three cats
I need the money
But it's not always enough
I smoke a lot of weed
It gets me through
But it's not always enough
I would be smoking every day
If I could afford it
And I don't write anything, anymore
At all

Her printing was perfect: sublime. I wonder who will find that one, she thought. Someone is going to buy that journal someday, maybe for half-price, and some girl is going to get it and draw and write poetry—maybe with a friend—or maybe just by herself. No one will ever see it. She'll fill the book and then she'll get to that poem and she'll be mad that she got a used journal or maybe she'll think it was a friend and be mad at them for ruining her book or maybe she'll think it's a ghost and be excited and buy an *Ouija* board and try to contact the ghost of the writer. If I am a ghost, Tania thought, if I am *that* ghost, I won't come when the *Ouija* board calls. Maybe, and more likely, she'll never even see it because she'll get about four pages into the journal and quit because she's a popular girl and she doesn't have to write poetry in a journal because she'll have friends and boyfriends and play volleyball and get a car for her birthday and the journal will turn up in a garage sale that her parents have twelve years after she got it and the cycle will start again with a new girl.

Tania went home and smoked her Saturday bowl, and it was harsh and it burned and it was fucking wonderful and she slept deeply and dreamlessly for twelve hours. When she got up, she fed the cats, restless with hunger and irritable, or possibly just filled with cat-ambition from their inscrutable feline dreams. The cats fed, and she smoked her Thursday bowl on Sunday night with the TV on and the sound off.

Forty-Five Minutes
of Unstoppable Rock

Ray won't have the radio on in the car when we are working, except for after the 12:00 news when the advertisements are done and they play an extended set of songs. "Forty-Five Minutes of Unstoppable Rock," they call it.

"I hate the radio these days," he told me, our first day on the job together. "Nothing but advertisements for auto insurance, credit counseling services, trustees in bankruptcy, and vocational training schools. The four horseman of the econo-pocalypse, fifteen to thirty seconds each, and as much as two minutes combined. No one needs that. And you know why they do it? Why advertisers buy radio time? It's because people lost their homes and live in their cars. They're trapped. Me? I just want to hear some music. I want to think about good times!" He laughed when he said it.

There is a lot of truth in what Ray said about radio. Such are the times we live in.

We drive and we talk.

"How's things with Sheila this fine California day?" he asks me.

"Not all that good."

"That bad?"

"She wants out. Or more accurately, she wants me out."

"You're shittin' me."

"I wish. I mean, she won't say 'It's over, pack up your shit and get out,' but she says things like 'Something has to change,' and 'We can't live like this for much longer,' and stuff like that. Truthfully? I think she just wants me to pull the trigger."

"So what are you going to do?"

"I don't know. I was thinking about it, and I'm going to suggest couples counseling. Maybe her benefits will pay for it. She has good benefits."

Sheila and I met when I was a title insurance rep. She worked in City Hall, in Records and Permits. I was pulling in $7,000 per month, standing in line in front of her with all the other reps once or twice a day. I felt good all the time. I wore my embroidered shirts untucked, and my jeans long, the hem down to the heel of my ostrich boots. I'd just throw the jeans out when the hems frayed and get some more. I wore aviator sunglasses inside. I wore them inside bars, inside restaurants, and inside the hallowed halls of the Department of Records and Permits. Never took off the shades. I thought it would be like this forever—I'd fly in a gentle upward trajectory to a permanently sunny apex. People wanted to buy, sellers could be found, and lenders made it rain. It was an auction. I had just bought a $340,000 condominium. Brand new. No one else had ever lived in it. Half the size of my parents' house and more than three times what they had paid. This was six months before Lehman Brothers was cremated. Six months after that, and the smoke of their burning still hung in the sky over all of us along with that of a whole lot of other financial institutions, and I sold my condo for $175,000 and moved in with Sheila. Thanks to a deficiency judgment, I am still paying on a condo I no longer own. I am in arrears on that. It has been tough.

"So you're hanging on for her benefits? While she hates you a little bit more every day?" Ray asked.

"Well, no, it's not like that."

"Well, asking her to ask her benefits to pay for counseling ain't exactly the Cowboy Way, neither."

"You know what? Call it what you will, Ray, I'm just trying to make things work. Ain't nothing wrong with that." When I am around Ray, I start to talk like him; I use his diction, his phrasing.

"Ain't nothing wrong with that—except that everything is wrong with that," he said.

I snort.

"Seriously," he says, "you don't understand women."

I shake my head. "And you do?"

"Yes, I do. Here's the deal: you go to a woman and say you want counseling, you want to make things work, you're so sorry about this or feel bad about that or you will try and do better—whatever. They think you are weak. They can't abide weak."

"How's trying everything to make a go of it weak? Tell me that, Cowboy."

"It just is. Look—women. They get their opinions from other women. Imagine a secret boardroom, and there is a tote board. Maybe it's one of those fancy whiteboards like what we have now, or maybe it's just a blackboard and chalk like in days gone by. It don't matter. There is Sheila and all the women she knows. Friends, enemies, in-betweens—her goddamn mother, too—all together now. They have a consensus. On that tote board, they have two columns: one is 'Names' and under it are the names of all of their men, and the other column is called 'Weakness.' Under 'Weakness' and beside each name is a description. 'He cried,' is one or 'He begged for forgiveness' is another, or hey: 'He said he'd never go to the strip club again.' All of those things and more. But right there at the top is 'Counseling,' only they don't call it 'Counseling,' they call it 'He wants me to pay for someone to do his crying, his begging, and his apologizing for him.' They adjust the board each meeting and laugh and laugh—and then they go home and turn the heat up. They want to see if you can finally grow a pair and get the fuck out. See if you can at least manage some pretension of dignity. Internally, she's already trained herself not to miss you anyway. And she ain't no different than any of the rest of 'em."

I roll my eyes. "OK Ray. What's your suggestion?"

"Break up with her first. Pull the goddamn trigger already. You should have done it six months ago."

"But I don't want to."

Now Ray's shaking his head at me. "That doesn't matter. Listen to yourself, man. Listen. You have already told me she's talking like it's over. So you gotta be the one to say it. The trick is to do it right, to get off of the top of their board. You gotta do it and let her know that it's her fault."

"What?"

I actually look at him. I run a yellow light that turns red halfway through. I hope they don't have a camera on this one. I can't fucking afford that. In that split-second, in that intersection under a red light, I realize why Sheila is tired of me. Because I cannot risk running a red.

"Tell her you are breaking up with her because she has gained weight. She's letting herself go."

I stop at the next red and look at him. Ray won't look at me. I look at him until the car behind honks and I look up to a green light and start moving again.

"Yes," Ray says, "weight. Hit her right where she lives. Women worry about that shit. She might roll her eyes, talk all sorts of crap but if you tell her she's letting herself go, looking a little dowdy—like someone's babushka-wearing grandma—and you can't be with her anymore— she'll be in the bathroom and on the scale the moment you are gone. She'll be crying in the mirror. You'll be off the board. 'Dumped me because I got fat' is the very last position on the board. Rock bottom. Makes *her* look bad, not *you*. Some of her friends will sympathize, some will gloat—her goddamn mother will say something unhelpful—but the point is this: you walk away with some pride."

"Weight," I say.

"Yep. Weight. Besides, it's probably true.

We all gain weight as we age. How long have you known her? If she isn't up ten or fifteen from when you met, I'll pay your red-light ticket."

It's quiet now. No radio. I have a lot to think about.

"Hey!" Ray says, "Ranchero Drive. Turn here and let's go take Mr. Echeverria's house."

We are in the 'bad news' business, or, more correctly, the 'more bad news' business. We are the black heart of the dark cloud. We are the worst day a person has after they think they have already had their worst day. In the state of California, the last stage of the foreclosure process is the "Notice to Leave After the House is Sold." You miss a mortgage payment, then another, and then it's three mortgage payments and you give up, quit, and the lender starts the process. The house is either sold and the new owners want in, or the bank is stuck with it—which is the last thing they want—and they have to get you out. Anyway, what happens is that the new owner must give the former homeowner something called a "Three-Day Notice to Quit (Leave)" and file an "Unlawful Detainer" lawsuit to evict.

That's when Ray and I come.

We come in a rental car, white or black or silver, and we bring with us the Notice to Quit and the lawsuit. Sometimes the houses are empty; the owner gone with the foreclosure notice. They slink away to another place to forget this place and these times, which is what I would do, but sometimes they are still there. Squatting I guess, because it must still feel like home. Mostly they just don't know where they are going to go. We deliver the bad news and we hope they take it well. We work in a pair because another guy at another firm—he got shot. Right on the doorstep. It made the news. One man was led away in handcuffs; another covered in a sheet and wheeled away on a gurney. No one wants to be the guy on the gurney. You can talk shit about "Foreclosure Mills" all you want, but someone has to do it, and the one I work for is not as bad as some others. They pay two of us; most places just send one. One person, in his or her own car, is pretty easy to fuck with. We are two of us, have a rental and haven't been shot yet. If life isn't good, it's less bad than it could be.

Hector Echeverria's house on Ranchero may or may not have Hector Echeverria, but he was getting his three days. We park across the street and look around. There aren't many people out. Some of the other houses on the street have the windows boarded over. They were the Echeverrias before our Echeverria. Always, Ray knocks on the door and I hand over the documents. I keep the Affidavit of Service in the car. We'll fill that out once we are back in the car. No one answers the knock. I put the papers in an envelope and stuff them in between the door and the doorframe. I've gotten good at it. We're walking back to the car when the garage door opens and there, behind us, with two suitcases and a lamp of the Virgin Mary holding an empty picture frame, is Mr. Echeverria.

"Can I help you?" he asks.

Ray answers, "Well, yes. Are you Hector Echeverria?"

"Yes," he says.

"Allow me to introduce myself. I am Ray Bevans and this is my associate—"

Echeverria waves him off.

"I know who you are. You are here for the house. It's OK. It's yours. I'm leaving now. I don't want any trouble."

"Well, we need to give you the documents. Can we at least do that?"

Echeverria shrugs. "I guess so. It makes no difference."

"Thank you, sir," Ray says. "You are right, it doesn't make much difference, but it's always best to do things by the book as much as possible."

Echeverria sets the lamp down and I hand him the Notice to Quit and the eviction suit. He tucks it under one arm and picks up the lamp and tucks it under the other then picks up his two suitcases and walks it out to the curb. He stops, then, and turns around and takes out the garage remote and closes the garage door.

"Here," he says to Ray, "take the opener. The new owners will need it. I was going to leave it in the mailbox."

"Thank you, sir," Ray says. He takes the opener.

Echeverria picks up his bags, his lamp, and our papers, and begins to walk down the street.

I'm relieved. No fuss, no muss, no gun,

no gurney. I like it best when the houses are empty, but I've had people get pretty heated. I understand but hey—they have to understand, too. We either serve 'em or join 'em. The line is razor thin.

Echeverria, not moving real fast, gets about one house away and Ray calls out to him. "Mr. Echeverria. Do you need anything?"

Echeverria stops for a moment but doesn't turn around. He starts moving again, but even slower.

"Mr. Echeverria, can we give you a ride at least?"

I look at Ray but he isn't looking at me. Jesus, Ray, don't do this. What for? Echeverria stops, but does not turn around.

"Mr. Echeverria. We can give you a ride. This other stuff? It's just our job. If you need a ride, you need a ride. Let us give you a ride. Where are you going?"

Echeverria stops and turns around. He looks long and hard—at Ray—not at me. "The bus station," he says. "Just the bus station. Can you do that?"

"Hell yes," Ray says. "That's 8 miles away. Hell of a walk. Way too far on a hot day. Let us give you a ride."

He motions me to get the car and he goes to help Echeverria with his bags. We get in the car, with me driving, Ray riding shotgun, and Echeverria in the back. Ray and Echeverria had put all of Echeverria's belongings in the back except for the Virgin Mary Lamp. Echeverria carries her with him and holds her on his lap; Mary in white and blue, with her sacred heart in red and gold, and her hands framing the empty picture frame.

"Where's that bus taking you, buddy?" Ray asks, after we begin to move.

"Indio," Echeverria says, "Indio. I have a cousin there. He'll put me up until I can find a way back to Nicaragua."

"That's cool. Is that where you are from?"

"Originally, yes."

"You have family?"

"My wife and her mother, her sisters."

"Well hey, something to look forward to, right?"

"Yes."

Echeverria looks straight ahead the whole time, neither at Ray nor at me. I keep looking back at the lamp using the rear-view mirror. I wonder where he found that. Maybe it came with him from Nicaragua.

"Whose picture was in the lamp?" I ask, "Your wife?"

"No," Echeverria says, "my son."

"Is he in Nicaragua with your wife?"

"No, he died."

Ray and I both say "I'm sorry for your loss" at the same time.

"Thank you," Echeverria says.

We get to the bus station and get out. "You need anything else?" Ray asks.

"No thanks. You have done enough. You have been very kind."

"Seriously, you need anything, you just say."

Echeverria picks up his bags and walks into the terminal without looking back.

"What was all that about?" I ask Ray when we get back in the car.

He turns on the radio and points at the clock: 12:20 p.m.

"Forty-Five Minutes of Unstoppable Rock. Time to turn up the radio."

<hr />

We do two more that afternoon. Fortunately, no one is at either house. I wedge the Notice to Quit and the eviction suit in the seams where the doors met the door frames and they hold tight. It's not as easy as it sounds. Some of these places in these cookie-cutter subdivisions were put up fast and cheap and there is often too much space between the door and frame and they will not hold the documents tight, so they fall to the ground and get rained on, or kicked around and messed up. No one likes that. It looks unprofessional. I try to look at the bright side and tell myself that the carpenter who installed/framed the doors is probably in foreclosure himself, or maybe even dead or in jail. Unemployed, at the very least.

It's the little things.

"Let's hit the strip club," Ray says to

me as we drive back. We are coming into peak commute time and he had turned the radio off a while ago.

"No thanks," I say.

"C'mon, you need it more than I do and my girlfriend is there. My girlfriend who actually likes me."

I grimace. "No."

"It's your call," he laughs.

"So who is your girlfriend now?" I ask. I can't resist.

"Ramona Raxx. That's 'Raxx' with two Xs."

"Seriously?"

"Seriously."

"What's her real name?"

"Well, Ramona for sure. She swears it's Ramona. She's holding out on her real last name. She told me she wanted Roxx—with two Xs—but it was taken."

"Oh it would be. That's a good one. But tell me this, Cowboy: what makes her your girlfriend?"

"She's sweet on me. I can tell. I know, I know. You think I'm bullshitting. But she's sweet on me and it's kind of charming."

I just look at him.

"She showed me her gunshot wound."

I laugh a bit too long at that. "So that's what they're calling it now?"

"No, no, no. She has an actual gunshot wound. I know. She showed me."

"You're kidding."

"No, I am not. You know, I went in there Monday. It's always slow. I don't sit up front on pervert row; I like to sit back, have a beverage, and check out the stable. She comes out, pretty little thing, real black hair and real white skin. And freckles. Those freckles are cute. All men like freckles. Don't say you don't. Anyway, she's up grinding it for the lost souls on pervert row and I can see this big gauze bandage above her bikini line and kind of off to one side. I'm intrigued. Admit it, you would be, too. So I tell the server to send her over to my booth for a little table dance when she's done up there on the stage.

She comes on over. She grinds. She's whiter up close, her hair blacker, and in the dead center of that bandage is a little red. 'Jesus, honey, you're bleeding!' I said. 'A little,' she said. 'What happened, baby?' I asked her. All she would say was that 'Some shit happened.' You know how it is. House party. Everybody high. Some guys were arguing and then shit got real, real fast and all of a sudden she was shot. It went through her side, in and out, like a hole-punch on a folded piece of paper. Just the right angle. Someone drove her to a hospital and dropped her off and she went in and told them she had no insurance but would they please help and they did.

"I kept her there for two more dances. During the second one, she peeled back the gauze and showed me the stitches. A little clear fluid was leaking out of her. She said it was a combination of plasma and the antibiotic. They had warned her. She was OK. She's a toughie, let me tell you. After that, we just sat and talked. She told me she was planning on leaving the Central Valley and going out to the Bakken."

"The Bakken?" I ask.

"Yeah. The Bakken Shale Formation.

Montana, South Dakota, Wyoming. Goddamn near all of those places and then some. The next oil boom. She told me some other girls were dancing out there and make a grand on a weeknight and more on the weekends. Some of those oil riggers haven't seen a woman in three months and they'll throw a whole paycheck's worth of cash money up there for just a kind word and the opportunity to stare at some pretty pink areola."

"It does sound good," I say.

"You know, after that she thanked me. She told me that she'd been shot on a Thursday and missed the weekend and all the good tips. Coming in Monday—and she had to beg the club to let her dance on Monday—she expected nothing. She told me my money was the difference between her making rent or couch surfing until she could find another situation. Times are tight for everyone. Even strippers. She told me to come on back and see her tonight."

"You sure she's not just working you?" I ask.

"Nope. I'm not sure. We'll see if she gives me her real last name. If she does—we'll know. But I have a good feeling. I've always been lucky, in small ways. Just like my daddy."

"How so?"

"Well, my dad is from South Dakota. Born there and died there. He cowboyed for real. Met my mom at a rodeo in Bakersfield. True story. That's where I was born. But California—and my momma—wasn't for him. He moved back out to South Dakota before I could even remember him. He was a cowboy there, a ranch hand. He liked it. Drove an old pick up and fished in his spare time. Catch and release. Never did hunt. 'Live and let live,' he always told me. He passed on a couple of years ago. Died while fishing. Must have had a heart attack or something. They found him just sitting there by a river. The current had pulled away his line and rod and they never did find it. It was the most expensive thing he owned and the last thing he did was give it to the river. It makes me feel good to think of it. My cousin, Mike, called me to tell me and I went on out to the funeral. I told my mom about it and she shrugged her shoulders and told me that my daddy was the luckiest man she ever knew. He wasn't rich-lucky, or famous-lucky, or even good-at-something-lucky. He just did what he wanted to do and lived easy. No one ever bothered him, or took that ease from him.

That's lucky."

"Amen to that," I say.

"Anyway, at the funeral, Cousin Mike told me he already had a couple of wells on his land and was looking to form an oilfield services company. He did it and now they are booming. I talk to him every so often and he always says, 'Come on out, we could use you.' So, tonight, if Ramona gives me her real last name, I'll tell her about Mike and my dad, and tell her that I, too, am going out to the Bakken. I'm going to shake off the Central Valley like an old memory and let it fade. This is going to be a place I used to be and that's all. If Ramona is in, she's in, and that would be great. My mom is in Fresno now; I'll come back for Christmas and that's it.

"Sounds like a plan," I say. "They have any decent radio out there?"

"Oh yeah!" he says. "The best. No depressing commercials. Not much in the way of advertising at all. Everyone does the same thing out there. They don't need to advertise. I noticed that when I was out for my dad's funeral. Forty-Five Minutes of Unstoppable Rock four times a day.

"We should all be so lucky," I say.

"That's the Bakken," he says. "Once I get established, I'm going to call you up. We could use a guy like you. I am sure of it. Just let me get out there and get going. Hell, I'll even look for Echeverria in Nicaragua. We could use him, too. He seemed all right. Not his fault that his kid died and that the market turned. Nothing he could do about it."

We park the rental on the lot and put the keys in the overnight return. We'll be back tomorrow. Back out to Stockton. To a house once owned by a man named Diaz. As for tonight, I'll go back and pick up Sheila from work and see what she has to say. I'll let her talk and if I don't like it, I'll just not listen. If she doesn't want to talk, that's OK, too.

June 25, 1977

"You are nothing like your father."

My mother would say this to me when we argued and certain things would come up. There are no hurts like an old hurt, no slights like the first slight. In an argument inside your mother's house, nothing is ever left unsaid. Nothing can be taken back, not with a word, not with a phrase.

"We are both good at math," I'd say.

She would clench her teeth and go do something away from me. I would go back to doing whatever I was doing that had upset her.

My father would come to see me on the last Saturday of every month and we'd spend the day together. Invariably our routine was the same. He'd greet my mother and me at the door. She would lock the front door and walk past him without saying a word. She'd get into her car with my Aunt Anne, her sister, and they'd go shopping. My dad would put his arm around me and walk me out to his car. He had a 1964 Chevrolet Impala Convertible. It was a lustrous black with a white interior. He'd inherited it from his father, my grandfather, even though we had not seen my grandfather in years. My dad took good care of it. He told me he only drove it on weekends, and often only on the Saturdays he came to see me. He told me he had also bought a Toyota. It was much better on gas and he drove that the rest of the time. He intended to keep the Impala, he said, but once he hit ten thousand miles on the odometer he was going to store it. "It'll be worth a lot of money to a collector someday."

I remember that car now, in my mind's eye, and I believe that to be true. It was a really beautiful car and worth keeping hidden away to be the privilege of a later generation, better able to appreciate it when there were fewer of them left.

We'd get in the Impala and go to his motel. My father would always come out Friday night after work. He was an electrical engineer. He worked for a defense contractor in Lancaster.

He worked long hours and would often be driving out after dark so he'd come out and get a motel room rather than try to come out first thing in the morning. He'd tell my mother we were going to a car show, or a ball game, or to where he worked to see the jets, but we'd go back to the motel first. He always booked a room with two beds; his clothes laid out on one, mine on the other. The last Saturday in June in 1977 was the last time we dressed together. He had laid out a cotton summer dress for himself, white polka dots on blue. He wore pantyhose with it. He always wore pantyhose. No amount of depilation could hide his legs. On that day they were nude in color, but I remember that on some days he wore white. He wore pearls too, and three rings—two on his right hand, platinum and white gold, and a silver one on his left. The silver ring was ancient; it had been his mother's and his grandmother's before her. The story in the family was that his grandfather had won it in a mining camp poker game in the late 1920s and had given it to her as an engagement ring. So my father wore these three rings and that one set of pearls and Chanel No. 5. The real thing, too. Perfume, and not Eau De Toilette. His eyeliner was very precise, his foundation broadly applied, and his lipstick very red.

Once he was done we would dress me. On this particular Saturday, he had brought a gingham dress, white and navy blue. It was sleeveless and very light. He had brought some sandals for me too—white, also very light.

Once I dressed, he stood me there in the half-light of the motel room with its heavy curtains drawn and made me turn around. He *tsk-ed* at my hands and feet and took me into the bathroom to clip my nails. I was in the habit of forgetting them. He had me wash my hands and feet before he trimmed them—he told me it softened the nails and made them easier to clip neatly—you don't want them to be too brittle and break off unevenly. He had worn driving gloves when he drove the Impala out to my mother's house and now that they were off I could see that he had nail polish on, a soft and muted red, more a plum, very rich and particular color compared to the overstated maraschino cherry of his lipstick. I perched there on one leg with one foot in the sink and did each foot in turn and he noted how tall I was getting and how I could do that now. He reminded me that there was a time when I could sit up on the counter beside the sink and soak both my hands and feet in the warm and soapy water all at the same time.

The hotel soap was strong-smelling, antiseptic, and I walked out with my hands and feet smelling of it with those white sandals on and my nails neat and I could just barely smell my father's Chanel underneath it all.

Once in the car, he put a scarf on over his head and put on sunglasses. He popped his lips to check his lipstick and started the car. He stopped before backing up and looked at me for a long time. "Here," he said, and while the car idled he took out his lipstick from his purse and put some on me. "You're old enough to wear a little. You don't need it, but it looks good. If you look good, you feel good." He blotted the edges of my mouth with a tissue and popped his lips again at me and I understood this to mean I should do the same and so I popped back.

He drove without his driving gloves then, his bare hands upon the wheel and the sun lightening his nail polish and we'd cruise a bit. He liked to drive. We would drive up and down the canyon once, looking at the houses, and sometimes we'd drive up in the Hollywood Hills. Sometimes we'd park up in the observatory parking lot and just sit there, looking down over the city. My father would adjust his clothing constantly while he talked to me. He'd tell me things about the city and how it used to be when he was growing up and even before he was born. He'd ask how I was doing in school. He took great pride in my math marks.

No matter what else we did we'd end the day with a trip to Phelps's Pharmacy. He'd drive us to Phelps's and he'd always turn off the radio and sing some doo-wop song he made up and if I wasn't singing with him he'd shout at me in between verses to join in.

> *Boom Sh-Boom*
> *She lights up the room*
> *Brightens Everyone's Day*
> *Boom Sh-Boom*

I'd move my head and shoulders with the music but I wouldn't, I couldn't, sing. I was shy in my own way. Shy when I was with him.

Phelps' was a relic even then. It still had a soda counter. An ancient man with a white apron and one of those little white paper hats tended the counter. He didn't have a name tag but my father always called him "Tony" and the old man always listened without speaking.

My father would order us two chocolate malts. Tony would make the malts and put whipped cream and a maraschino cherry on top of each. While Tony was making our malts, my father would fidget with his clothes or his pearls and tell me that Lana Turner, a famous actress, was discovered at a counter just like this. She was buying a coke at a pharmacy soda counter and someone saw her and the rest is history. "But don't worry," he'd say, "that's not going to happen to us," and he'd wink at me and his eyes were a little too bright and his red mouth took the malt off of his spoon while he looked at me. My father had very brown eyes. Almost black. We'd eat our malts and I'd set my cherry aside. I didn't like them.

We would eat our malts in silence, nursing them for a bit and then we got up to leave and Tony came over to clean up after us. "You two ladies have a wonderful day, now," he'd say, without inflection. Tony moved slowly, arthritically. There was rarely anyone else in there. My father reapplied his lipstick in the car and helped me to reapply mine, which I did without much enthusiasm. We went back to the motel. It was almost five o'clock when we got there. My father took off his dress and his rings and pearls, and showered. I imagine he took his make-up off in the shower. I undressed while he was in the bathroom, laying the dress out neatly, putting the sandals on the floor beneath the dress, and putting on my shorts and T-shirt and then my socks and runners. I remember having those Nike runners with the "waffle" soles and being very pleased with them. I loved to look at my footprints in dirt or wet ground.

My father would get out of the shower and dress and pack quickly, putting my dress and sandals in his small suitcase, and we'd leave. He had a brief moment of panic when he could not find his driving gloves, until he remembered that he had left them on the seat of the Impala.

On the way back to my mother's he handed me a broadsheet from a car show with a list of vehicles and the names of their owners. "Tell your mother you liked the Corvettes best. The '65s and '66s especially." He dropped me off without getting out himself, and he'd watch me go all the way into the house. My mother would always be in the kitchen; she was never at the door. I could hear my father singing as he pulled away:

Boom Sh-Boom

She lights up the Room

My mother greeted me in the kitchen. "Did your father feed you?"

"Yes," I said, "but I'm hungry again."

She looked at me closely and came over. "What's this on your mouth?" She held me by the chin.

I had forgotten to take off the lipstick, my father's lipstick that he had put on me at the motel. I popped my lips involuntarily and my hand went to my mouth.

"We had maraschino cherries on our malts after the car show," I said, "That must be it."

My mother went to the sink and got a washcloth and ran it under some warm water. She came back over and washed the maraschino red off of my mouth without saying another word. I looked away from her and out the kitchen window and tried to think about nothing.

Boom Sh-Boom

I sang in my head.

The following Monday, I came home from school and my mother told me that she had enrolled me in soccer. I was old enough and it would be good for me. She knew I liked soccer. Games were Saturdays. "What about Daddy?" I asked, "Do I still go with him on the last Saturday of the month?"

"No," she said, her back to me. "He can come and watch you play baseball. I have discussed it with him and he thinks you should play soccer, too."

She bought me cleats and I liked them even more than my Nike waffle-soles. I'd walk out on the field and when I crossed from the grass to the dirt I'd look back at the neat impressions left by the cleats.

My father came on the last Saturday of July and watched me play. He sat by himself, with the other team's parents. My mother and my aunt Anne sat on our side. After the game he came up and put an arm around me and told me that I'd played well and that he was really proud of me. I showed him my cleats and the impressions that they made in the ground and he seemed to like them, too. I asked if we were going to go get a malt or something and he apologized, said that he needed to get back into the city, and that he had not brought the Impala anyway; he had been afraid it might rain.

He came to the last game of the summer, on the last Saturday of August. He sat by himself again. He had a black eye and a red scrape on his forehead.

"What happened to you?" I asked after the game.

He looked at me and his eyes seemed very dark and very sad.

"Nothing," he said. "A silly accident. Nothing to brag about."

He told me I had played well and that he was proud of me. He admired my cleats again. He had driven his Toyota again and I asked him if he thought it might rain on him on the way back.

"Not at all," he said. "The Impala has crossed 10,000 miles. I bought a cover for it and it's in the garage."

He put his arm around me and squeezed me firmly. Underneath the odor of my own sweat, baseball glove oil, and mown grass drying in the sun, I could smell the faintest hint of his Chanel.

That was the last time I ever saw him.

My father moved to Seattle in September. He'd gotten a position with another defense contractor. Cards came, birthdays and Christmas, and cash. I grew up, fought with my mother a lot, and moved out when I went to school. My marks, my marks that I talked with my father about up at the observatory on days so sunny they could only be in California, were always good. The cards quit coming, and I lost touch.

My mother died of lung cancer, of menthols, of vodka, and sitting. At her funeral I asked my Aunt Anne if anyone had thought to tell my father. She just looked at me. A few days later she came over with a manila envelope. "Someone should have shown you this a long time ago," she said.

My father had died ten years before my mother. He had been found naked at the bottom of a motel swimming pool in Key West, Florida. There was an examiner's report. The autopsy showed his blood alcohol to be 0.22—almost three times the legal limit. The report noted his age, his height, and his weight and I remember being surprised at how small he was. He was not a large man at all, this man, my father. It noted that he had no birthmarks, significant scars, or identifying marks, save that at the time of his passing; he was found in the pool wearing red nail polish.

I knew that had to be wrong. "Red" was not quite right. It would have been dark, more of a plum color and not something bright and plastic that "red" implied. Aubergine? Yes, aubergine. I forget where I learned the word, but I knew where I had first seen the color called aubergine. Yes, aubergine. It suited him better than "red."

"Death by Misadventure" was the opinion of the examiner. My father had gotten drunk and drowned. I don't know if there was more to it than that. I do not want to believe that there was, but the report seems too simple to be correct. It had no nuance, no insight. It was to his passing what red is to aubergine.

No one had claimed his body. In accordance with the laws of the state of Florida at the time, he was cremated and interred in a municipal cemetery in a plot marked with a number.

I put the things back in the folder and returned it to my Aunt Anne.

"He did have life insurance," she told me. "Your mother was the beneficiary. Even after all their years apart. I suppose it was his way of looking after you."

"Do you remember his car? The convertible? The black Impala?"

"I do," she said. "Vaguely. The one he inherited from his father, your grandfather?"

"Yes. Do you know what happened to it? Did he have a will? A list of his possessions? There was nothing in the envelope."

She shook her head. If it wasn't found in the folder then it wasn't to be found at all.

I wonder what happened to the car. I imagine it parked up in the observatory lot on a cloudless summer afternoon, looking as new as the day it was purchased. The sun shines and the chrome and vinyl gleam and I can smell the heat coming off of the engine and underneath that, the faintest hint of perfume.

Bruiser

Mondays are good days. Wrestling is on TV.

It's going to be hot today. The sun is a hammer; the pavement, an anvil. I'm going to go pick up stray dogs, then prowl Wal-Mart looking for unlocked cars. When I find one I'll put the dog in, lock it up, and walk away to imagine the rescue attempt—or the no-rescue attempt. Sometimes no one notices.

I am the hand, the instrument that delivers the message. I am not the author. Or maybe I am. I wonder if it is even possible to know.

I hope I find a Chihuahua. They are easy to handle and hard to feel sorry for.

I get lucky. I get a Chihuahua. She is just behind a chain-link fence in her yard, dragging her nose in a slow, arthritic trip around the border of her little domain. The fence is only three feet high. That's ridiculous. It's an old lady's fence for an old lady's dog. I just reach on over and pick the old girl up.

"How old are you, girl?" I ask her out loud while rubbing her chin.

She just shivers and looks around and away, the way that dogs do. Her eyes are bulbous, darting. That's part of the reason I hate Chihuahuas. That and their personalities.

I keep her in the crook of my elbow so that she can brace her paws on my arm. Dogs do not like being off of the earth. They are animals and want four feet on solid ground. With no feet on the ground, they are like a box with the top cut off, unsupported, and so made weak. Being made weak, they become afraid.

"Let's go to Wal-Mart," I say. I sound positive. I'm not faking it either, because I am pleased, and dogs don't understand your words, just your tone. So I sound positive. I don't want to scare her.

We walk away from the yard and the too-short chain link fence with the whitewashed metal posts, just like that.

I am lucky twice today it seems. I have found an unlocked vehicle—an old pick up, black on black. It has a topper, too, so it's impossible to see into the cab from the back. I set the Chihuahua on the seat and she looks at me, eye to eye, for the first time.

"Sit," I say, calmly and with authority. Tone is everything.

Her eyes bulge and she shivers but she sits and she stays.

The cab smells of cigarette smoke and gasoline. Somewhere something leaks. There's a half a jug of windshield wiper wash on the floor of the passenger side and a dream catcher hangs from the rearview mirror. Someone has been through the reservation. Probably filled 'er up and bought the dream catcher. I bet there are fireworks and a jerry can with five gallons in the bed, under the topper. Maybe even a rifle rolled inside a blanket, but I don't have time to look. It's an old truck, and the owner left the windows slightly open for ventilation, so I grab the handles and I crank the windows up tighter than tight. I lock the driver's side door and then the passenger side and then shut them firmly. I have to wipe my brow as I get out and step back. It's already hot. Triple digit high today, I bet. The Chihuahua looks at me with those little bug eyes and is already panting hard.

I walk away, not too slow, not too fast. Don't want to linger, don't want to run. I brush the thought of the dog off of my shoulder, the same way my mother would have. Her learned gesture is my inheritance. I brush and I don't look back.

———

I was six years old and my mother and I were walking back home from witnessing door-to-door for our faith. We walked across the pedestrian bridge alongside the overpass. Homeless men sometimes lived under the overpass, especially in the summer. Mother always held my hand a bit tighter. They frightened my mother and although she never said as much, I could feel her fear in the grip of her hand on mine whenever we would see them.

On this particular day, we had crossed

the bridge when three of the men came up, black, bearded, smelling of sleeplessness and wine and the smoke of a fire made from broken pallets, and carrying a fourth man. He was ruddy-cheeked and blue-eyed. He had a long beard, a honey-brown color streaked with grey. He clutched his chest and coughed and rattled and his eyes watered. They placed him on the sidewalk and then walked back down without looking back. He died of a heart attack while we just stood there looking at him.

My mother brushed her shoulder, brushed it all off like she was taught to do, then brushed mine and led me home. Dirt off our shoulders.

The next time we witnessed we went the same way but there were no men at all. I remember being a bit surprised—I thought we'd see the man lying there. The other men had very deliberately set him down away from their camp and their fire. I knew they wouldn't move him. I wondered who had taken him? Who looks after these things?

My mother never mentioned it ever.

Monday night wrestling means TV dinner on a TV tray and the Elbow of God.

My favorite wrestler is the Priest of Pain. When he finishes off the unworthy, the unrighteous, or the merely unruly—heels or jobbers, *jabronis*, all of them—he climbs the ropes and descends upon them from that great height with the Elbow of God to finish the match. When he singlehandedly defeated the Kentucky Klone Klan (three overall-wearing, steel-toed-boot-clad, bearded giants, all named Kletus), in a "Loser Leaves Town" match, he ascended the ropes three times and three times came down, dropping God's elbow on one Klone at a time, each in his turn. Then he knelt and said a brief prayer over their twitching and insensible bulks before their manager and the other heels came in to cart them off in an old ambulance. It was pure pandemonium in front of seven hundred screaming fans in the arena, and God only knows how many like me watching on local-access cable.

I love the Priest.

I also love Salisbury steak with carrots, peas, mashed potatoes and gravy. The apple cobbler I could take or leave. Dessert is for the weak. I've tried other TV dinners but nothing else can compare. Especially the gravy. It needs the Salisbury steak to make it all work, or so I figure.

Some nights I have two TV dinners, but if I do I fast the next day.

I don't have cable anymore. I don't have TV. I haven't since Mother passed. But I have my VHS tapes and our VCR. Monday's still Monday, so I heat up my TV dinner in the oven (just one today because it's so hot), and put in my tape *The Priest vs. The Kentucky Klone Klan* again. I watch this at least once each month, and sometimes more if I'm feeling down. But I also have *The Priest vs. Li Kang Gong* (supposedly the former official executioner for Pu Yi, the last Emperor of China), *The Priest vs. King Coffin* (really, a tall wrestler in a Halloween skeleton costume and top hat with a silver skull buckle that concealed "voodoo powder"), and the rare *The Priest vs. Adolf Squared*—another set of clones (the idea was so good it worked twice)—in a "razor match." Here, the Priest shaves off the moustaches of the clones with a holy straight razor after a furious battle, the outcome of which was much in doubt for quite some time. The match was held in Brazil. The referees were corrupt, and mysteriously spoke only German. But still: the Priest.

I know all of his matches by heart.

The Universal Champion's Wrestling League folded a few years back and I have since lost track of the Priest. It seems reasonable that he would have retired, rested upon his laurels with his championship belts and the memories of his many victories. But in my mind, I see him continuing his ministry of strength overseas, perhaps in the Philippines, the Japans, or even the Punjab—places where they have a wrestling culture and might be prepared to hear his word even as he drops his elbow from up atop the ropes.

***

It's definitely not a two-dinner night now. Way too hot. Even with the heat and some hours between us, I can still smell the gas and cigarettes in the cab of that truck too. It takes the edge off my appetite.

The timer on the oven rings and my Salisbury steak dinner is ready. It's time to watch wrestling.

Mondays are the best days.

All of the Words to All of the Songs

I have never known the love of a good woman. I have only known the temporary affections of a few bad ones.

Her name is Denise. When she was small she could not pronounce it correctly, so her stepdad nicknamed her "Dancey" because that's how she pronounced it. I always called her "Dancey," but I always referred to her as "Denise."

"I believe in God now," I said, and I meant it.

She laughed.

"You are like, the thousandth guy I've blown, so I should be good at it."

I said nothing.

She laughed again.

*"Well, more like half that. Might as well be
a thousand though. I used to drink a lot. Every
night after work I'd hit the bar. It was a party all
the time. Somewhere, anywhere. Who can count
everything? Who wants to?"*

*She got up and went into the bathroom.
I lie there in a mathematical silence, counting
glasses of wine in my head, dividing by the
number of days in a year, in a week, and then
multiplying, then adding, then losing track and
starting again.*

Leap years, fuck, what about leap years?

My cousin Mike picks me up in his truck.
Dancey had emailed to say she'd left my stuff
in a box on her step. She said to come and get
it while she was at work. If it's not there when
I get there, it's stolen—the neighbor's kids are
assholes—and not to ask her again. I'd emailed
back to tell her to put this and that in the box—
just to make sure she remembered—but the
email bounced back. She'd already closed that
account.

"You up for this?" He asks.

"I'm up for it."

"If you just give me the address, I'll go get it."

"I'm good. I should be the one to get it."

"You want breakfast?"

"McDonald's would be good."

We stop at McDonald's.

"Don't worry, I'll get it'" he says.

Mike goes in. There are no drive-thrus here among the palm trees. There is actually a bylaw. It's a resort town full of retirees, cue-tips, constipated blue-hairs, people dying expensively slow; drive-thrus offend their collective sensibility, their class's idea of class. No one here works, except for the ignored. These are the people behind counters, or under hard hats. They work while the walking cadavers complain and golf and nap. Once they can't golf anymore, they just sit. They want to die warm, and the climate obliges.

"Remember who loves you," I said.

"Can't you just say 'I love you?'" she replied.

"That would be something everyone says. I don't want to say things, the important things, the same way everyone else does."

"I just want what everyone else gets."

"McDonald's coffee is actually pretty fucking good."

We're in the truck, eating our breakfast sandwiches and drinking our coffee. Mike is actually right about the coffee—it is pretty fucking good. Too bad we can't get it at a drive-thru window like every other place in the world. Out here in the desert, two hours from LA, and four from Vegas or Phoenix, the gentry make their own rules to no one's convenience but their own.

We get to Dancey's and there is a lizard on the white stucco wall of the townhouse, brown and still. At the end of the driveway there is a roadrunner. The roadrunner has seen the lizard on the wall. The lizard knows. The roadrunner wheels away with that peculiar gait they have—

the cartoons aren't wrong—only leaving once we step out of the truck.

There is not a cloud in the sky. There is no box on the step.

"Asshole neighbor kids took my stuff," I say.

"Are you sure?" Mike says. "Maybe it's off to the side."

We look around a bit, even inside the gate to the condo's pool. It's early in the morning so no one is at the pool yet. There is nothing there. We can look into Dancey's little yard from there. There is nothing there.

"Maybe she's just fucking with you, man," Mike says quietly.

"No," I say, "It was kids. Fuck it. Let's go."

We get back in the truck.

"I always felt it said something that her own kid won't live with her," Mike said. "You know what family law is like. 'Mother's house, father's income.' And yet..."

I shrug and we go.

The lizard is off the wall, gone to someplace

else now to wait out the heat of the day and hide away from the roadrunner's gaze.

She always fell asleep with the TV on. The "ID" channel. "Murder porn," I called it. "Yep," she'd say, "Murder porn." Every night. After she fell asleep, she'd wake up and check her phone. She'd do this at least two or three times a night. She'd wake up and it would wake me up. One time I said, "C'mon baby, put the phone down for a bit and come on over and let me put an arm around you."

She got up.

"I don't like the way you said that."

She went out to the couch and turned on the TV. I could hear her crying.

I looked at the ceiling fan turning slowly around and around and listened to her cry under the murmur of the TV and eventually I fell back to sleep.

"What all did you lose in the box?" Mike asks.

"Just some personal shit," I say, "and my DVD of *Conan the Barbarian*."

"The greatest movie of all time!" Mike says. "I mean that. I'll get you another copy myself, even if I have to steal it."

I nod. Thank God for Arnold crushing his enemies, driving them before him, and hearing the lamentations of the women. In the length of time it takes to hear that line in my mind, I don't think about Dancey.

When we get back to my place we just sit in the truck for a while.

"Do you want to go to Vegas?" Mike asks.

I shake my head.

"LA? We can go into LA if you want. Let's go out to the pier. Redondo even. Less crowded. We can get lunch on the pier and watch some old fuckers fish."

"I'll be all right."

"OK man, but if you aren't better by next weekend, we're going to Vegas."

"Thanks Mike."

I get out of the car and start walking

in. There is a lizard on my stucco, too, yellow-brown, like sand, and big-eyed, alert.

Mike backs up, stops, and leans out the window. "Next weekend I'm going to Vegas, with or without you!"

I half-smile and walk in. The lizard runs for the shadows around the corner and is gone.

Van Halen played on the radio. She told me, "Van Halen played my high school before they were called Van Halen. There's a picture in my yearbook."

I started to sing "Dance the Night Away" and she took over from me and finished it singing every verse and chorus in turn, a little slower and a little sweeter than Van Halen's own recording, and it made me think that this was the way that the song should be sung. She had a softness to her voice, a purity, beautiful like her handwriting, and I believed her about the band playing her high school. But I told her that "everyone knows that song," and I asked, "Do you know any others?"

"Try me," she said.

I'd name one song after another and she'd lie there with her head on my shoulder and sing them, a little down tempo like she had "Dance the Night Away," and every song I named, she knew exactly. I even threw out "Never Had a Lot to Lose," and she looked up at me and raised her eyebrow and said "That's a Cheap Trick song," and then she sang it, too, chorus and verse, in that voice, her voice, her head on my shoulder looking away.

When I first told her that I loved her I told her over the phone. I said "I love you," just like anyone else would, just that one time. So when I told her, "remember who loves you," it was always like everyone else says "I love you;" I was just referencing that first time. Like it will feel that way forever. But I never told her that. I never thought of explaining it that way until after it was over.

Why do things have to end?

Because they have to end.

It is never *what is* that beats you. It's thinking about *what should have been*. When you are young, you are soft until the first cut, and when you are old, your scars rub against their scars, no matter how carefully you lie down beside one another, and you open up and bleed again.

I think of the lizards on the walls, holding their breath to be still against the overwhelming white, and of Van Halen on the radio, and of how she knew all of the words to all of the songs. Maybe next weekend I will go to Vegas with Mike, or go into Redondo for lunch on the pier and watch the old men fish. I could go to Phoenix for a ball game with the kids. It doesn't really matter. There will be a long and perfect drive with the radio on, playing all of the songs I know, lullabies a little slower and a little sweeter than ever they were before.

Broke

Oil is around forty dollars per barrel and I haven't worked in eight months. I'm driving to my parents in a truck that I'm ninety days behind on to borrow money from them.

I have four texts on my phone: the first is from my old boss getting back to me saying he doesn't have anything for me and doesn't know when he will and things are bad all over. The next three are from my ex-wife and all about money I owe her.

- *You owe me around three thousand dollars.*

- *For Trina. The money is for Trina.*

- *Can you give us anything? It doesn't have to be all of it.*

Trina is my daughter. Support is the entitlement of the child. I am not arguing. I'm just not responding.

I pull into my parents' driveway. They have a house and three acres that's been paid out for years, and my dad has his teacher's pension. He always said he did OK for a cowboy's son. It is true. My granddaddy cowboyed on the Mackenzie Ranch. The Bar-Mack. Famous in its time and notable even now. My parents have a picture of him, on the bookshelf, with his horse and his dogs. It's an old black & white, and Granddad looks happy, and his horse, indifferent, dogs everywhere around their legs.

My mom asks me how I am doing. I know she is asking about money.

I'm doing all right, I say.

Dad is in town, getting an oil change, so I sit down and wait. I look up at Granddad's picture. All the dogs are greyhounds, except for one. It's an Irish wolfhound. The greyhounds all mill around Granddad, ears and tails up, looking at him, but the wolfhound is looking down and away, thinking about something else. He's with the pack, but not part of it. Different.

I'd like to have this picture, Mom, when you're done with it.

You can have it now. Just take it.

She seems irritated.

I don't have to have it now, I say. It looks good where it is.

I'm sorry, she says. It's not you, or the picture.

What is it?

Well, your dad isn't here so I might as well tell you, but you can't say anything to anyone. Least of all, your dad.

I nod.

She goes on and tells me that a few days ago, Dad had taken some old wood out to the landfill and had come back, no fuss no muss. Well, a half-hour later he gets a call from Willard Frame saying Dad had hit his fence—what was Dad going to do about it?

Willard lives on a country corner where you turn to go down the landfill road and damned if he hadn't built his fence out right to the road. It had been hit before, by others, by people pulling trailers or with stuff for the landfill hanging out the backs of trucks, and Willard has made a supplementary income from getting money out of people for fence repairs. Move your goddamn fence back they'd say, but Ol' Willard kept it right where it was. There wasn't a by-law or statute that applied out there. For a time, Willard ran the landfill, too, but eventually the county contracted it out to some big company and all Willard has now is his fence.

Did Dad hit the fence, I ask?

He says not, Mom answers.

Tell Willard to go pound sand then.

He says he's got estimates, written estimates. $2,900 dollars for repair and replacement.

That's not proof Dad did it. Tell him to go to court.

Mom cocks her head and looks at me with one eyebrow raised.

Your Dad already told him that.

It's true: Willard doesn't ever go to court. You can stare him down that way and see what happens. There will be sugar in your gas tank, or antifreeze for your dog. Have you ever seen a dog die after drinking antifreeze? It kills their liver and then kills them three very painful days later. They look at you the whole time.

Do something, do something.

They say it with their eyes.

Do something. Please.

They don't understand why you can't do anything. It won't cost $2,900 to have the vet put your dog down, but Ol' Willard will have got his.

Willard called six times yesterday, Mom says.

I look at my Granddaddy's picture. He never owed anyone anything and never missed a bill. Same for my dad.

Have you got any blank envelopes? I ask her.

She gets me a blank envelope.

What's that for?

Can I use the phone?

She hands me the phone.

I look through the caller ID and see all the calls from "W. Frame" and hit call. Willard answers

Yep, he says. That's how he answers the phone.

I tell him who I am, that I am calling on behalf of my dad about the fence.

$2,900, he says. I got estimates. Written estimates. You and your dad are welcome to read 'em over.

Yeah, we could do that, I say, but why don't I just cash you out and we'll call it done.

I'm listening, he says.

$1,500, I offer.

No way, he says.

Look Willard, you and I both know you ain't gonna get the fence done. You need the cash. If you want to get it done, you can buy the materials then wait a month or two. Once the harvest is in you can get some Mennonite kid, some farmhand, to do all the labor for you for $250 and a case of beer. Everything else is money in your pocket. $1,500. Either that or don't fix it—keep it all. I don't care. I got $1,500 to do this. That's what it is. $1,500.

Willard waits a bit, as if he wants me to think he's seriously debating it.

Deal, he says.

Like a deal was ever in doubt. I could have made him go away for a grand. It isn't Willard's first rodeo.

You know my dad's place, I say. If you can be here in a half-hour, I'll hand you a check.

I'll be there, he says.

He hangs up without another word. Mom opens up:

I can't write Willard a check for $1,500 without your dad here.

I don't want you to.

You can't write him a check.

She knows I'm broke. I know I'm broke. Everyone knows I'm broke.

I am not writing him a check.

What are you going to do?

Stay inside.

What are you going to do?

I stand up and fold the envelope in half, put it in my back pocket under my empty wallet.

My parents have a long driveway that can hold four trucks or six cars. My dad's garage is at a right angle to the house. I go in through the door and then raise the garage door farthest from the house. My dad has a little workbench in there where he works on his odds and ends of projects. He is not a finishing carpenter, not at all, but it gives him something to do. Right now he's building a little melamine shelf. What for I don't know. But there it is. I take his claw hammer from where it hangs from the peg-board. It's one of those thick foam-handled ones, a longer handle than most. I think it's actually a framing hammer, but I'm not a carpenter either. When you get older you need a little more leverage to drive a nail; the longer handle of the framing hammer gives you that much more leverage, a little more applied force. You can drive a three-and-a-half inch nail with one tap with a framing hammer. It's easier on your wrists and hands over time, too. I take the hammer and the melamine shelf my dad is building and go outside the garage door and sit on the shelf and set the hammer by my side and wait for Willard to show.

There's a story about Willard, how about

one time he went into the co-op to dispute a bill for seventy-five dollars or so—he brought in a receipt for payment for the amount he'd been billed. This was back when the co-op still hand-wrote all receipts. I forget her name but someone's grandma worked the counter there— and she was a tough old bird. She took the receipt Willard brought her and was pretty sure it had been altered. She pulled down a calendar off of the wall and spoke to Willard matter-of-fact:

Now see here, Mr. Frame, you have a receipt here for the 24th of the month in question but that can't be; the 24th was a Sunday. We aren't open Sundays. Do you want to address this with Clark, the manager?

Willard asked for his receipt back and she gave it to him. He walked back out and never mentioned it again. Still buys from the co-op. Some people think she should have turned over that receipt to the manger and then to the police, but I think giving Willard his receipt back saved her dog. And you know it isn't the first time, or the first place, where Willard took a ballpoint pen and changed a "1" to a "4" or something like that.

Sitting on my dad's little melamine shelf with the folded envelope in my pocket and the framing hammer beside me, I take out my phone and text my ex-wife:

- *I'll have it for you by the weekend. Tell Trina her Daddy loves her.*

Willard pulls up in his old two-tone Chevy picky up. White and blue with a topper. Have you ever noticed how every crook—and every guy over sixty—if they've got a truck, it's got a topper? He's been running that truck for twenty years. His kind of small-town graft must not pay all that well. I see he's got one of his kids in the passenger seat. He's a little blond guy who doesn't look anything like Willard. I wonder: why would he bring his kid along to cheat another guy out of money? But as soon as I think that, I think: of course he'd bring his kid along. That's Willard.

I stand up and take the folded envelope out of my back pocket and hold it in my left hand. I pick up my dad's hammer with my right. Willard gets out of the truck. Willard is one of those guys who is around 5'7" and runs a deuce-and-a-half minimum. He's built a lot like my ex-wife, actually. He's almost perfectly round, as wide as he is tall. One of those aggressive bellies—all fat but firm, hard even, pushy. He's wearing jeans with suspenders because guys with that build can't fit a belt right. He has on a black T-shirt, ball cap, and sunglasses. He always wears sunglasses. He's got construction boots on but no laces; men shaped like Willard need something they can slip into. He isn't made for tying up laces.

I hear you got a check for me, he says.

I hold out the folded, empty envelope with my left hand. He reaches for it with his right and then holds it up to pull out the check he thinks is in there. I hit him with the hammer—sidearm swing—quick as you can. He's looking at the envelope the whole time and I catch him right in the side of his lying liar mouth and a handful of his teeth fly like hail against the wall of my dad's white stucco garage, chased by dark red blood thick like cream. The teeth rattle on the wall but the blood is too heavy and falls short and onto the little melamine shelf in an un-pattern like those strange paintings rich people call art.

Willard's lost his sunglasses now, and his hat. He looks at me and I can tell he's surprised.

I jack him again—overhand this time—that long-handled hammer with its titanium striking surface leaving a perfect round impression in the dead centre of his forehead and he's down, falling sideways and then rolling onto his back. He keeps his left hand on his mouth. I don't stop. Twice, I swung that hammer like an anvil on a chain, picking my spots, and I break up his face. The strikes, at first perfect circles—dents of crushed bone—are starting to swell, to hematoma—and he looks like a Hollywood horror. He's bubbling up, changing color. The whole goddamn time he kept that envelope in his right hand. Even now, with him unconscious on his back, out of his boots and breathing out bubbles of blood from the shorn off roots of his teeth, he holds on tight.

Willard, you crooked piece of shit, I say. There's your fucking check.

I wonder if Willard even knows that my parents don't have a dog.

<hr>

I look up from Willard and see his kid, open-mouthed and wide-eyed, staring at me from the truck.

You. Get out of the truck, now, I say.

He dives down and I can hear him locking the doors. I walk over and look through the window and see him curling up in a ball on the floor.

Open the door, I say.

I'm not yelling; I'm not loud.

Just open the door. I won't hurt you.

He doesn't open the door, so I swing hard and fast with my dad's hammer and I smash the window. If hammers have souls, somehow imbued by being a thing made, a thing created like we are, my dad's hammer is having the best day a hammer ever had.

Willard left the truck running and there is country music on the radio. Country music is for non-Catholics, people without truth and reconciliation. It's full of bad behavior and self-righteousness. Y'all go on and do bad things but keep your chin up because hey, you love your country and other people done treated your tender little heart bad. It gives you a license to be a shit. I know. I grew up listening to that stuff and you know what? Some of it I don't even mind.

The kid whimpers the whole time. I unlock the door and tell him to get out, but he just stays in a little ball and whimpers. I drag him out by the arm but when I let him go he just falls to the ground in a little ball. Poor kid.

Stand up, I say. I'm not going to hurt you.

Somehow he stands up.

Stay right here, I tell him.

He stays, looking down at the ground and shaking. It isn't cold out. After laying about Willard's face and neck with two-plus pounds of framing hammer, I'm getting a bit sweaty. The kid's just scared. I understand.

I set the hammer down on the bloody melamine shelf and go on and get the little jerry can my dad keeps for the lawnmower. I pour some gas over the kid, over his head and shoulders and then set it back down. He's making odd sounds now. He's choking with fear.

Look, I tell him. I said I wasn't going hurt you and I'm not. Not now. But you know gas burns right? Gas makes fire?

He stands with his arms crossed and shakes. He doesn't say anything. The tears, big tears, they come down off his cheeks and hit the ground like his daddy's teeth. His little shorts are wet, soaked. I didn't pour that much gas on him.

Again, I ain't going to hurt you. Not today. I know you understand me. I know you know that gas makes fire.

He's moaning a bit now. Mm-mm-mm-mm-mm. Like that.

Your daddy is going to wake up in a bit. He's not going to feel real good. I'll help you get him into the truck and he's going to drive you home. When you get home, your daddy is not going to say anything to your momma. He's just going to go lie down for a few days. Your momma is going to ask you what happened. She's going to ask you why you smell like gas. She's going to be scared, too.

I stop for a moment and take a deep breath. I like the smell of gas. Always have. Octane is good. The more the merrier. People should buy more. I take it all in. The kid is breathing heavy, too. He's soaked in enough gas that you can't even smell the urine over it.

You tell her that your daddy tried to steal

something. I caught him doing it. And that if ever I see your daddy again, even once, I'm going to set you on fire. I'm going to set you on fire, I'm going to set your momma on fire, and I'm going to set your brothers and sisters on fire. I'm going to set everyone on fire, from the oldest to the littlest ittiest-bittiest baby in the house. She'll smell the gas on you and she'll know I mean it. Do you have a dog?

He still won't talk. I give up.

DO YOU HAVE A FUCKING DOG?

He finally looks up at me. He even stops shaking. We see eye-to-eye.

Yes, he says. Yes we do.

I'll set the dog on fire first. You can all watch before I set you on fire. Now get back in the truck and wait for your daddy.

He gets back in and curls up down on the floorboards again, the country music on the radio singing songs about bad men and good women, or vice-versa, or flags on the porch or the cousin you lost your virginity to, or who the fuck knows.

Willard doesn't look to be coming around

anytime soon so I go back into my dad's garage and wipe down the hammer and put it away, wipe down the melamine shelf, and lastly take a push broom and push Willard's teeth out onto the road. I should have made the kid do it but he smells like gas and he has already peed his pants.

Everything done, I sit back down on the shelf and check my phone. No new messages. Nothing to do but wait for Willard to leave and for my dad to come back so I can go sit down with my parents and beg them for money.

I can't imagine my dad, or my granddad, ever asking anyone for money.

I'm so broke.

I drive away from my parents' home with a check and the picture.

My granddad cowboyed for the Bar-Mack back in the '30s, during the Great Depression. No one had any money. Wages were hard to come by and even when you had paying work, the wages might keep you fed and housed or they might not. But they paid a bounty on coyotes in those days, five dollars per pelt.

That was good money then. So that's why my granddad got his pack. He'd run coyotes from horseback with that pack of greyhounds and they'd run the coyote down, pin it in a gully or in some scrub, something like that, and hold it at bay. Coyotes are what I call stupid-smart. Can't stay away from the calves but they'll run along the fence line and under the barbed wire and slalom through the fence posts. The grey hounds will run along either side of the fence and take that away, but they can't kill a coyote, not one at a time or even all of them at once. Not easily anyway. Coyotes will kill. Cornered, they grow fiercer by despair, and it's a real fight. That's where the Irish wolfhound came in. That wolfhound could run with the greyhounds and run with the horse, all day long. When the pack brought that coyote to bay, the wolfhound would move on in and kill it, take it by the neck and hold onto to it until it was dead twice over. Granddad would get down from his horse only once he was sure the coyote was dead and skin it in a flash before the rest of the dogs tore it to pieces and rendered the pelt unsalvageable. He needed the five dollars and it was paid only on the whole pelt. He called the wolfhound his "Killing Dog." It knew how to kill; it was bred in him. I think that's why he stands on his own in that picture, set apart as it were, in the pack but not of it. He was something else.

Cold Enough to See Our Breath

If I die in February: Scatter my ashes, then smash the urn.

This is what he wrote. I believe that he would do the same for me.

The trail to the river's edge is bordered by deadfall and small stones and marked with deer droppings and the paw prints of coyotes. Even by their track, you can see that they are lean and hungry, and think of nothing other than their empty bellies. It's almost March but it'll still be dark by five and you will able to hear them keen and wail like they have never seen fire.

It's actually against the law to dispose of anyone's remains, even their cremated remains, in the waters of a national park, but that's where he wanted to go, so we are going to do it. Some cemeteries have an urn garden where cremation lots are available for burial of an urn. Others have a columbarium: an above-ground structure where urns are held. Another option is to bury the cremated remains in a family plot. Some cemeteries also offer a common scattering garden. If you think about this, these are options for the convenience of the survivors of the deceased, those of his flesh and bone, but not of his spirit. They are really there for those worst of all human beings, the Godly, those who collect tolls from the bereaved.

What I mean to say: If he wants wind and water—we'll give him wind and water.

Hurry, Mary said, it's going to be dark.

Think about what we are doing, Mike responded to her, No need to rush.

I carried the urn and the ashes. Together, the ashes—pulverized to silt—and the ceramic urn weighed almost ten pounds. Who would have thought? I read once that the heart, a tough, fibrous piece of muscle, is the last thing to burn. I asked the guy at the crematorium if this was true and he said it wasn't—that at the temperatures used, everything burns at the same rate.

What about in the old days, I asked, The Vikings and their funeral pyres? Their burning long ships with their hoary kings and strangled wives?

I don't know about that, he said.

He did not smile, or hazard a guess, or look at me when he answered.

It's two miles from the parking lot to the river's edge. I was not sure about Mary, but I bet Mike was sweating and I knew I was.

We should say something, Mary said.

We waited for someone to speak. Me, his ex-classmate, Mike his former co-worker, and Mary, his ex-wife.

Mike spoke first:

I know Dan's dad committed suicide. He used one of those old Webleys—the British Navy revolvers. I think it may have fired a small cannonball. That's how the conspirators killed Rasputin; never mind all that talk of poison and drowning and shocking amputations. A Webley. All he ever told me was that on his seventeenth birthday he found his dad, in the garden shed with a hole the size of a man's fist from the exit wound in one side of his head. It was big enough to see through. The bullet had gone through the thin plywood wall of the shed, too, leaving a hole big enough to see into the shed. His dad had a Bible beside him, a glass of good Irish whiskey—untouched—and the Webley. He said he never blamed his father for the suicide but never forgave him for doing it on his birthday. The old man never left a note, so no one knows why. After his dad's funeral, Dan came home with kerosene, a match, and a rake, and still in his suit, he burnt down the garden shed and raked the embers into ash until it was level and cold and the last spark fled into the dark. It took him six hours. He finished just before midnight. He said he didn't know what he was thinking, only that it is what he felt he had to do.

I handed Mike the urn and he uncapped it and shook it so that some ashes went into the air in a long arc before drifting off the edge of the river, down into the almost frozen water below.

He handed the urn back to me.

Mary spoke next:

When Dan was twenty-one, he was bitten by a rattlesnake while he was out hunting deer. He was bitten on the thin part of his calf right above the ankle. He showed me the scar, and truthfully, we were married, so I saw it often enough. He and I were used to it. "All it did was hurt," was all he told me. "No real damage." He also told me that every seven years or so, in October, around the anniversary of the original bite, it swelled and pained him again almost as bad as the first time. I never saw this with my own eyes—we weren't together long enough. Once we got divorced, I never saw him for eight years, and when I did see him the first thing he told me, after I had said "Hi," was that I had come back, just after the seventh year, to pain him again. He laughed when he said it, but I could tell that he hurt a little, too.

Mary was quiet and I handed her the urn. She shook out some more ashes on the slow-moving water, blue-black in the fading light, and then handed the urn back to me.

I thought a minute, and then shook out the remaining ashes, far and wide and wild. They fell farther out into the dark water and sparkled in the setting sun, dancing like familiar sprits. What do I know? I had not talked to him for twenty years. I did not know their stories. I could not remember making this promise—I think we had been drinking. But here I am, in February. I took the urn overhead and flung it down upon the rocks that lined the river as hard as I could, and it smashed, smashed, and scattered into a hundred pieces. Any not cast into the river by the force of my throw, I kicked in with my foot. Mike and Mary stood back, closer together now, and said nothing. In the silence, we heard the first short, insistent bark of a coyote, nearer to us than you might think, but still on the other side of the river. She called again, and again, but no answer came back from her sisters.

He wanted wind and water, I said, so I gave him wind and water. Rest in peace, Dan, buddy. That's all.

<hr />

We walked back in the settling dark sun along the trail by the coyote and her gathering sisters, farther and farther away from us with each step.

At the end of it, I think, when all is said and done, no one knows you by your last wishes, or even the stories they tell about you, or by the chants and incantations of wild things looking at you from the shadows cast by trees. As for a promise made to another man at another time, it is better not to think about it, just to do it. Scatter the ashes and smash the urn like he asked, where he asked, and there it ends, and maybe you will know yourself a bit better, or maybe you won't.

We walked on from February's passing and towards March's inception, away from him and away from the water, the wind, the shadows of the trees, and the keening sisters, with the air now cold enough to see our breath.

Shirlena

I will now speak of the Devil.

In appearance, the Prince of Darkness presents a compact figure, between five-foot-six inches in height and six-foot even. I am inexact, I know, but he is no closer to the former than to the latter. If I had to guess, I'd say five-nine, but this is just my impression and not an exact measurement. He is of average build, perhaps "athletic" more than "muscular," spare and firm without being hard. Some men become well-formed by hard labor and others by their own efforts at the forge of sport, but a lucky few are born blessed with an inheritance of their parent's superior proportions. In this regard, his Dark Majesty has an even superior genesis. His facial features are symmetrical and perfect, his youth undeniable, his hair immaculate. His skin, his beautiful skin, is unblemished, save in but one regard: he has a small red spot, more mark than mole, just beneath the corner of his left eye. From one angle it seems to make him look a little sad; from another, consumed with anger; and from another yet, he will seem both weary and benevolent at the same time. I cannot do more than to suggest these as possibilities because only he and the one who laid that mark upon him know what it means. But it must mean something, right? Nothing of his infernal presence is accidental. His eye color? I cannot remember. It is immaterial.

More than the way he looked, I remember the way he smelled. Not of sulfur, nor of fire, nor of brimstone (which I have never smelled), and certainly not of excrement or filth or the rotting flesh of the grave. Nothing of the sort. I believe that his body, the form that he had chosen for the moment (save for the red mark of course) carried no odor at all other than perhaps that of sweet, sweet youth. But I know without a doubt that when we parted company for this second and last time, his breath smelled unmistakably and strongly of bleach, and that the smell of it clung to him like a shut-out loss.

I was not curious. I already know how this shit goes.

So when he came back this second

time—a second time after promising there would only be the one—I was unimpressed. Been there, done that. Silently he came in and silently he stood, his hands in his pockets, waiting. He stood behind me so that to converse, I had to turn to look at him. It is his way of imposing his will. You always have to turn to him. Upon my left hand was the drink Terri had made me— made me special—and as I had already declined it twice it seemed only proper and fitting that I offer it to him.

"As a courtesy," I said, without looking back at him.

"Don't mind if I do," was all he said, and as his breath escaped with the words I smelled the bleach. I do not know that bleach would kill a mortal man, nor how it should affect Satan himself, who was born of God's own word, but I knew it could not have been good. He drank the Reach-Around all in one shot, and set the empty glass down upon the counter at my left hand.

"As a courtesy," he said, with a slight pause before continuing, "I left her in a small place, very far away where you will not find her."

And with that he was gone. I looked to

my left and behind but he was not there. The old-timer at the end of the bar gestured to the mirror again and nodded knowingly, holding up two fingers. "Twice," he mouthed at me, "Twice."

The air did not move with his departure and I assumed that he had vanished into the space and time of his infernal domain, but then in the stillness I heard the faintest sound from the lot across the street, the sound of metal on the thin plastic veneer of red automotive paint.

I do not think Terri saw him this time.

Johnny Camaro's gonna be pissed. Double pissed actually.

Some things are harder to explain than others.

You know how that shit goes.

So I leave the trailer and all I can think of is that it's my fucking trailer and I should not have to leave. It's my fuckin' trailer. She should fuckin' leave. Fuck. What are we fighting about? What are we always fighting about? It's Shirlena, so whatever it is, it's always a fight. She does not need a reason. More of the same or something different, the paths may vary but the destination is always the same. And if I don't like it, I can leave. So I do. Not for the first time, either, but by God, I swear it's the last.

There are no steps from the back door out to the parking pad. There used to be, but the last time that I left for the last time, I discovered upon my return that Shirlena had taken a crowbar to the boards that made up the steps and had torn them out and set them in a pile in the driveway. She then burnt them to black ashes.

I guess she was mad.

Even now if you look, you can see a stain where the fire was. I wonder if it was the kerosene that she used to set the fire that left this stain. She used the kerosene from the camp-stove to start the fire and then left the camp stove to be blackened and ruined in the blaze as well. Now I have no camp stove. Goddamn. My mother gave it to me for Christmas the year before. She thought we might like to go camping. Well, we can't now. Not without a camp stove.

I have to jump down from the landing to the ground, then walk across the driveway across the stain from the fire. I do not shut the door—she can shut it or leave it open, I am so mad I do not care. Each place, the missing steps and the stain from the kerosene fire is a monument to the insults I have had to endure. Try getting into that place at night.

I get into the El Camino. The El Camino is the finest automobile ever made. Everyone knows. My El Camino is a '72, and yes it has the SS package and it used to have a 454 in it, too, but some previous owner took it out a long time ago and I run a 350 in it now. The 350 is great, but getting a little worn and someday, someday when I have the money, I am putting a 454 back in, an LS7, 454 cubic inches, no more, no less. Someday, but not soon. I get into her, into the black vinyl driver's seat worn down to the springs. When I turn the key in the ignition, there is nothing at all. Not even a spark. I rest my weary head on the steering wheel for a moment but I know how this goes, so I pop the hood release and walk on out and open up the hood and reattach the spark plug wires to the distributor. She has done it before. It's not a sophisticated tactic. I can put the plug wires back in place in the dark now, no problem, faster than you would think. Practice makes perfect and God knows I have had to practice. Back in the driver's seat, I turn the key and she fires up—fire being the operative word. The sound is wonderful. The sound is the sound of movement and movement always feels like freedom. Last year I hid some money from her and got some new headers. I would have held off until I got the 454 and done it all at once, but that's a lot of money and I can only hide so much. When I hit the road, I already feel better.

Whenever I leave Shirlena, there are only two places that I can go: Texas Tom's or my mom's. Texas Tom's is my go-to bar. It used to be an Irish pub, but some guy who had gotten a little scratch together in the patch bought it because he wanted a cheap place to drink. Not a nice place—a cheap place. The sign outside used to be a leprechaun, but the owner himself had painted a cowboy hat on top of the leprechaun (he wasn't going to pay for a new sign) and named the place both for himself and for the state of his origin. And lest you think that I am critical let me say this: we are all grateful to him. By "we" I mean the crew. The guys from my crew are always there. When we are not working (which isn't often lately; the patch has been good and it looks like this time the boom will stay boom and never go bust) we are at Texas Tom's. Texas Tom's has nothing else to recommend it, save that it is close. A guy died in there once—went into the bathroom and never came out. No one noticed until the morning when the cleaners came. He had gone in there, had a stroke or a heart attack or something like that while standing in front of the urinal, dropped to his knees with his pecker in his hands and his chin in the urinal, an unlit cigarette in his mouth, and that's how they found him in the morning. There he was, hanging by his chin, propped up just so. Terri, the owner's wife/girlfriend/whatever/something, who looks after the place, told the fellas and we all laughed about it. Really, we laughed—I mean we fell about the place. That poor bastard, I wonder if he died with his eyes open or closed. And he was wearing a Broncos hat. Shameful! Anyway, to make a long story short, the cleaners called her, she called the cops, the cops called the paramedics, the paramedics came and said it wasn't their gig, they only pick them up if they are still flexible enough to you know, be possibly maybe restored to life, so the paramedics called the funeral home. The funeral home guys (who were very decent about it) came and picked up the stiff. Even under the sheet, you could see the odd outline of the body and you knew he was holding his pecker. It seemed kind of undignified until they got him in the hearse and the doors closed and everyone's equilibrium was restored. Once the funeral home guys were gone, Terri fired the cleaners. It's like on the rigs: if someone gets killed, the whole crew is fired. Safety is everyone's responsibility, so if someone...goes... everyone goes. One could suggest that the cleaners weren't really responsible—I mean, it's not like the guy drowned, but Terri is the only employee of the bar and as I noted, her position is more akin to owner than employee and the cleaners were the only crew she had. So she had to fire them. There is a higher morality that applies here. No doubt you understand.

I know that if I go to Texas Tom's, the fellas will likely be there, along with a couple of the video poker jockeys that might as well be getting in line for the honor of being next to die in the can. You gotta put in your time to die like that.

Ah, fuck it.

I do not need Texas Tom's. I have put in too much time lately. If none of the fellas are in there, I risk winding up at one of the video poker machines, the days will blur one into the other, and I am just waiting to die and be mocked. You already know how that shit goes.

I go to my mom's.

My mom lives in a condominium, a nice one. The thing you have to understand about mom is that she raised me up all on her own. She worked and worked and worked. She had no help from anyone. I never knew my dad, and I never knew my grandparents. I never heard her complain. She waitressed, she cooked, she cleaned for other people, she answered phones at a call center for the phone company. Other jobs, too. I cannot remember them all. She worked 7 days a week, 363 days a year. She only ever took off Christmas Day and New Year's Day, and then only because everyone else (mostly) did. In this day and age, the way things are now, she would have probably worked some on those days, too. She was never ever fired or laid off. And although I was too young to remember it, she worked enough so that she was able to buy the trailer—the trailer I live in now—and that is where I grew up. I lacked for nothing, I had no complaints. She never had any boyfriends while I was growing up; later in life, I once asked her about it and whether or not it might not have been easier having a man around and she told me that I was the only man she ever needed. After I had finished high school (she cried, the only time I ever saw her cry, because she was so happy for me—you know, she quit high school to have me) she met Earl, who hired me on for his seismic crew. Earl was a good man. He treated Mom well. My mom's name is Merlene, but Earl always called Mom "Merlie." No one else was ever that informal with Mom—she was polite to everyone but friendly to no one. Except Earl. I know they loved each other and I know they respected each other. Earl once told me that in the South, they often say "It's a wise man who knows who his daddy is, but it's a wiser man who knows who his momma is." One day, after I had been on Earl's crew for two full years and he made me line-boss of my own crew, Mom and Earl sat down with me in the trailer and told me that Earl had bought a condominium and that Mom was moving in with him. The trailer—the only home I had ever known—well they were gonna rent to me for reasonable. Real reasonable, it turned out. Was I excited? Damn right I was. I was not yet 21 and I had my own trailer! I had never lacked for anything, I had never held any complaints. Life was good.

And so it went on for a few years. I moved on and up in the patch, and eventually became a construction supervisor and left Earl's company. Earl was getting on a bit by then. He sold his company and planned his retirement with great enthusiasm. He was even thinking of buying a hunting cabin in Montana. Or a golf cabin in Montana. Or just a place in the mountains in Montana. Then he got pancreatic cancer and he died—died in pain—within ten months of the diagnosis. There is nothing fair about this life. Earl left everything to Mom. Mom never complained, but the whole thing aged her a bit. She still lives in the condo; I still live in the trailer. I still work, but Momma doesn't. She'd worked a lifetime already. Now she is a retired lady. She never worked a day after Earl came home and told her what the doctor said. She looked over Earl until the day he died. Even in the last days in the hospital, she did for him what the nurses would do except that she would not let them. She and Earl never bought that cabin in Montana. I was working a lot then, and didn't see them much in the last days. I just worked and Mom took care of things. Earl was a good man and those were good years.

All this was before I met Shirlena.

The El Camino and I roll on up to Mom's. I always park on the street, never in the driveway. Earl always insisted Mom get the garage, in case it got cold. I always left the driveway open for Earl's truck. Still do. Civilization is built upon such small measures of respect. Although I have a key, I always knock if I know she is there. The key is only to get in when she isn't there, when she is gone and I come to pick up the mail or water the plants or leave some cash. The cash is not for her—she doesn't need it—but I sometimes (often) have need to hide a small amount of walking-around money from Shirlena. God forbid I should be caught with cash on hand. So I knock. Civilization is built upon such small measures of respect. Mom greets me at the door, always happy to see me. But her smile only lasts as long as she sees my face.

"Oh Daniel," she says, sincere in her empathy for my misery, "Problems with Shirlena again?"

I can only nod because my voice might crack with anger or with tears if I dare to speak, so she leads me by the hand to the kitchen table and I sit. I have cried in front of my mom before. She said that I never cried as a boy. She sits across from me, and waits. She doesn't ask, she doesn't demand. She doesn't pre-empt my misery with criticism of its cause. She just waits for me to say whatever it is I have to say whenever I am ready to say it. I love my mom. She makes coffee for us, and then we sit while it cools. Eventually I am ready to talk. When I am confident, my voice won't crack.

"You can stay here for as long as you like," is the next thing she says, calm and reasonable, a lullaby.

"I know," is all I can say. "Thanks."

"Do you need any money?" she asks.

"Yeah," I say. "Maybe I'll get a hotel, or maybe I'll hit Tom's."

Mom gets up to get the envelope in the cabinet above the fridge. I have an envelope with some cash up there. It's my emergency fund. Mom calls it the "getting the hell away from Shirlena" fund. Back when I first worked seismic, my per diem was always paid to me in cash. I learned to keep it close and spend "under" it like a good boy should. It was one of Earl's lessons that I should always take the per diem in cash, whenever I could. If that was not possible, have it paid separately. "If it is paid by direct deposit, it's like it isn't even yours," he told me. "Sometimes a man needs to have a bit of cash in his pockets." Earl had been divorced many years ago, before he met my mom. It wasn't until I met Shirlena that I understood why he thought this was a good idea. Right now, everything goes direct deposit, and Shirlena can track every damn dime of it. The fellas have me half-convinced to go independent and set up my own company. Technically, I would be a sub-contractor to the company I work for now. The idea is that I can create a fictional employee and pay him a per diem in cash, but it would be me that spends it. I am sure there are probably twenty-seven things wrong with this scheme, and that the tax-man will arrive in ill humor for those who try to do this, but I understand its appeal. Oh yes, I understand its appeal.

Mom brings the envelope and sets it in front of me. I take $200. A man who has less than $200 in cash on him at any time feels like that much less of a man. And really, it's not much. Bar money and that's about it. You can't flee for your life on $200.

"Don't go back; stay here," Mom says, her voice still soft, but more urgent now. She can count as well as I can.

"Don't want to be any trouble, Mom," is all I can mumble, "You have done enough already."

"Shhhhhh," she says. "You were always a good boy, Daniel. Always. No trouble to me or anyone else. Never a day went by that I didn't thank God that you were so easy to raise. You are honest and hard-working, and I know it wasn't easy. And I know you deserve better."

"No, Mom," I cut her off, "it's not as bad as that. I can work it out myself. I have to have a plan. She has a temper. You know?"

"No!" she says, now it's her turn to interrupt. "I have a temper, Earl had a temper, but Shirlena is just mean. Crazy mean. You have no temper and that's why you won't stick up for yourself. When she turns mean, you just leave, and then you go back when you think she's less mean. You feel sorry for her, you feel like you should look out for her, you feel you should take care of her—but she's just mean. It is just wrong! And besides, you could have done better!"

"Mom, Mom, Mom." I say, but not too loud;

we are not arguing, "That's pure speculation."

But Mom is quick off the mark. She had her favorites. "What about that Anita that worked for Dr. Pepper?"

"I hate Dr. Pepper, Mom," I say, because it's true. I hate Dr. Pepper. It tastes like ass if you ask me. I remember Anita, too. Out of my league. I am not ashamed of having been raised in a trailer. Actually, as I remember, her upbringing was probably worse. Rented trailers. But Anita deserved better. I will not say this to my mom.

"She was not for me, Mom," is what I do say.

But Mom is not stopped. "That's no reason. If you hate Dr. Pepper, you can drink Cherry Coke instead. What about that Danielle that you liked that I used to work with, back at the diner? She was nice."

"She went to school to become a teacher, Mom; she was too smart for me." I know Mom will want to argue that. No woman is too smart or too good looking for any mother's son. But Danielle was smart and as beautiful as the morning sun, too. She could do better, too.

Actually, I think I had a better chance with Anita. And I had no chance there.

Mom argues it with her silence and her expression. Her expression says "I can't help you if you can't help yourself," but what she winds up saying is "Daniel, you always have a place here. I'll sell the trailer, I'll have the Sheriff evict Shirlena if she won't just pack up and go, and we will take it from there."

I say nothing at first. I know, I know, I have a place to go. *Places* to go, actually. But Shirlena—I just don't know about that. It might be her own fault. For sure, no one would feel sorry for her, but I can't just throw her out on the street. This has got to be done the right way, to minimize damage. I do not want to make her look like the victim. Also, I just think it's better if she pulls the chute.

The thing with the trailer is this: my mom still holds title to it. But it's "my" trailer, all right? At least this is how I think of it. I pay the utilities and the fees and take care of it. (Memo to self: rebuild the steps), but my mom still holds title. In return, I pay no rent. This is better than ownership and it makes it mine to my way of thinking. I mean, I live there, damn it. I have always lived there. I have never lived anywhere else. Shirlena knows about the title—it was the cause of our first fight. After she had been moved in for a couple of days (I had asked her to move in, I admit it) she had gone down to the land title's office and checked out the title. When I got home, she met me at the door, kissed me hard and wet, pulling my face towards her with one hand around the back of my neck like she had done every day prior to that and then in the same motion throwing an uppercut to my sternum so hard it left me breathless. That was a first. It hurt for days—there is no muscle there to absorb the blow. I wonder where she learned how do to this or if it was just that she had a natural instinct as to how to best cause pain. I know she was trying to hit me in the face, but she was too short. Man, she got me good. Higher—or lower—and she would have got me worse. With me on my knees on the floor, she said "I thought you said this was your trailer you lying sack of shit. Now I find out it's your mom's. Good thing I checked. Now get the hell out!"

I guess she was mad about the title.

I told no one of this. I cannot see involving my mom with this. She is too good of a person. It is not her problem. And Shirlena knows a thing or two about fighting eviction, believe you me. I heard from some of her previous landlords. I paid off her debts to some of her previous landlords. Apparently, she never paid anything other than first and last month's. And I do not believe for a minute that all of her previous landlords came forward. She had moved a lot, I guess. It's just best for all if she leaves on her own.

Coffee at Mom's place is not the way to handle this. I'll go to Tom's, then home to deal with Shirlena. After all, it's my fucking trailer.

"Thanks for the coffee, Mom," I say. I get up and go.

"Take care, Daniel," is her good-bye. "You are a good boy."

My mom has a way of calming me down. I am in a good mood when I pull in to Texas Tom's. I am in a better mood when I see the vehicles parked outside. Marty is here, from my crew; "Million Dollar Marty" we call him because he hits Vegas four times per year and always comes back and says he won at blackjack. If Marty is here, Thumper will be with him. Thumper's real name is Harlan; we call him Thumper because a few years back he took up with a nice Baptist woman and started attending church. Thumper is short for "Bible Thumper." Harlan and the Baptist lady broke it off, but the nickname stuck. "I'll give up dancin'!" he said, "and I'll let 'em damn near drown me in the goddamn river as many times as they like, but I'll be good and goddamned if I'll give up drinkin'!" Those were his exact words. Good thing, too, because before he was "Thumper," he was "The Colonel" after the chicken restaurant guy and he never did like that. It's like early parole when you get to exchange a nickname you hate for another one. Johnny B. is here, too; his truck is outside. His dad, "Johnny Senior," worked for Earl back in the day and rather than "Junior" and "Senior," we had "Johnny A." and "Johnny B." Much smarter sounding, don't you think? Parked across the street, at an angle across two spaces ("so as I don't get door dings") is Johnny Camaro's Camaro, so I know he's here, too. Any guy who angle parks across two stalls is by definition an asshole, but Johnny respects and admires the El Camino, so I tolerate his parking without comment and sympathize with him for the occasional keying he gets.

It feels good to be walking in to see the fellas. I walk in and Terri greets me with "Those other losers are at the usual spot; you had best get on out in case what they got is contagious!" and I know she will bring me my brand without me having to say. I sit down without saying a word and wait for the inevitable.

"Shirlena throw your ass out again, boss?" Thumper is the first in. I know by the way he says it that he doesn't know whether to laugh or buy. The fellas are all looking at me.

"Hey," I say, "can't a guy hit his favorite bar for a frosty cold bottle of his favorite brew with the guys?"

It's quiet for a breath—two breaths.

"Well yeah, yeah..." Johnny B says, "A guy could—a regular guy, but not a guy who lives with Shirlena. What's up, boss?"

Johnny Camaro is in before I can respond. "If she fucked with the El Camino—IF SHE FUCKED WITH THE EL CAMINO..." He takes a deep breath, then a second. "Boss, let me tell you—no jury would convict!" He takes a pull of his beer and he has a faraway look.

I look at Johnny Camaro with that look

you give to those crazy street people who are asking for money but are wanting permission to be crazy. "No, Johnny," I say, "she didn't fuck with the El Camino." For all he knows it's true—I have never told them about the stuff she pulls with the El Camino. Looking at Johnny Camaro, I know now why I keep that shit to myself. I mean, it's good to have friends but in the distant future I have no desire for Johnny Camaro to be telling people "Oh yeah, Danny Davis. We did time together, some murder conspiracy thing. Total Bullshit! TOTAL FUCKING BULLSHIT! Fuck that Fucking judge! He's next! And if I were to make a long story short you would understand. Danny's good peeps. Used to have this beautiful '72 El Camino, real sweet..."

You understand.

Pretty much every jury would convict.

I can only wonder how far this kind of shit will go. But Johnny shouting, "...SHE FUCKED WITH THE EL CAMINO!" is in my head, I must admit.

"So marry her," Marty says, leaning forward, finally coming in with his two cents. "You have lived together for some time now— make it legal." But it's not a statement; it's a question.

I take a deep breath and a pull at my beer, then a second. "No. No. No. That's out of the question. I have to tell you fellas, I think we are done. Shirlena and I are done. I know we are done."

"Jesus!" Johnny B. says, "Well that is too bad. I really and truly feel sorry for you." Johnny B. knows to say the right thing. His dad, Johnny A., was the same way. "What happened?"

"Well, what can I say?" is what I say. "It's neither here nor there or this or that, but sometimes two people just can't work it out, just can't make a go of it. It's nobody's fault, it's just the way it is." I even believe it when I say it. I am a practiced liar in this regard. The fellas? They are like kids. If we had kids, I would be telling the kids the same thing. "We tried, but..." I don't want to lie. I just don't want to tell the truth. I have my pride.

"No, no, no!" Marty says, interrupting my mental rehearsal. "No one splits because 'they can't make a go of it!' They split because he's an alcoholic, she's a crack fiend, or she cheated with his brother—or his boss—or he cheated with the babysitter—or the babysitter's mom—

or she spent the money on video poker, or he spent it at Texas Hold 'Em. Or, or, or. But not because 'we couldn't make a go of it.' Fuck me, man, practically everyone knows that practically everybody 'can't make a go of it.' The question is: why can't you make a go of it? Did she hit you with a fire extinguisher again?"

Fuckin' Marty has to bring up the fire extinguisher thing—which the fellas call the "per diem incident." To make a long story short (and therefore less physically painful), Shirlena found out about me stashing my per diem at my mom's and greeted me at the door with one of those little extinguishers, like what you keep in the kitchen for grease fires. She pitched it at me, overhand with a lot of leg drive, at about—how should I say this? At just below waist height. As I had noted before, her instinct for injury is refined.

I guess she was angry about the per diem.

Fortunately, I was able to block it, and only had a cracked bone in my wrist to show for it. I was still hot about it the next day at work (fortunately, emergency was not busy and I was fixed up good and quick and made a point of not missing any work over it) and I kind-of-sort-of told the fellas what happened and that that was why I was leaving Shirlena. Anyway, I am not making excuses for her for the per diem incident, but I decided at that time to give her another chance.

Somehow, I am on my third beer. We talk about not much; talking like that is like being quiet. But I know it will come back up.

"Well, what are you gonna do, boss?" asks Johnny B. "Something's got to give."

It's not a statement; it's a question. Fate hangs in the balance. Fate on a cosmic scale for me, nothing has ever been bigger. Somehow, I am on my fourth beer.

"I am going to go home. And I...and I...I am gonna dump that bitch!" That is what I say. I am furious at the beginning of my sentence, beaten by the end of it, and too quiet to be believed but the fellas can't tell. Either that or they mistake my whisper for commitment. They slap my shoulder, shake my hand, and try to be calm not knowing if they should be excited for me or play it straight.

"Like it's a bad thing. It's about fucking time!" Johnny Camaro says. "I swear she fucking keyed my Camaro once!"

"Just don't come back engaged!" Thumper says. He's been there before, engaged. Him, you have to take seriously. Somehow these things happen. He once told me that the closest he came to marrying the Baptist lady was when he was driving away for the last time.

I leave my fifth beer on the table. I don't want it. Five beers, the El Camino on the road, and my hands wet upon the wheel with the sweat of fear and my mouth dry with my anger and the cops everywhere and Shirlena at the end of the road with a fire extinguisher maybe.

You know how that shit will go.

I leave the last beer.

I drive, drive, drive, and by turns I am furious and calm. I obey the speed limit; in fact, I drive under it at all times, but I miss the lights and signs. I am a dangerous man. It is spring, warm during the day but cool at night, and as the sky cools the flying insects come out to seek the last heat of the day. They cluster and swarm around the streetlights and the reflection off their wings makes them look like sparks, a furious corona surrounding an unforgiving and unmoving star.

I met her in an all-night Laundromat. She had a black eye. I saw that black eye and wondered who could do such a thing? I felt bad. I felt ashamed of my gender. Some things are always wrong. I used to take two sets of clothing with me to the site we were at—I would wear one on the weekend and wash the weekday set in the Laundromat. I never bothered to take a laundry basket or even a garbage bag; I'd just sit and read a paper while the other one washed and dried. I had other clothes at the trailer, and my suit that I kept at my mom's. Shirlena had a laundry basket but nothing in it. I felt so bad for her. The Laundromat was in this speck of a town of less than 1,000 souls. I have never been back there. We were the only two people in there. When I was done, I asked her if she needed help. She shook her head no. It was after midnight. I sat by her and talked to her until the first light of pre-dawn, blue and cold, appeared in the eastern sky. She never said a word. When the sun had fully risen, an Indian woman came in with a huge basket of laundry. I thought it was a sign of some kind. I stood up and told her she was coming with me. She looked at me for this first time, eye to eye, and then she got up and came with me. I walked her out to the truck and went to hold her hand in mine. "I'm not a little kid," was what she said—the first thing I remember her saying, and she put the basket she had brought with her into the trash bin and got in the passenger seat. I was looking at her. She had on a blue T-shirt and shorts and sandals. She was not beautiful. Her cheekbones were low and round, her mouth small. She wore no make-up. She had piles and piles of hair of no specific shade of brown, with a very pronounced gray streak beginning at the left side of her forehead and going all the way back. She was a little overweight, not plump, not chubby, just…a little overweight. Nothing really.

"Don't you want your basket?" I asked

"Don't worry, it's not mine."

That was the second thing she said. We have been together (more or less) ever since.

I was happy then, when she first moved in, happy thinking that I had helped her and that she would come around. She never told me how she had gotten the black eye. She never talked about her past. She just moved in and day by day kind of organized things her way. She and my mom did not like each other from the start. She did not cook; she did not clean. She watched TV. If I was gone working, she cooked for herself. But she did not clean. When I got back, I would collect the dishes from the couch cushions and put them in the dishwasher. She smoked in the trailer when I was gone but not if I was there. This was her one concession to me. We never discussed it in formal language but this was the one thing she would not do while I was in the trailer and all understood it. For all of her apparent callousness, she was not particularly deceitful or sneaky. When the mail came, she would hold each and every piece up to the light to see what it was. Junk mail she opened—she read it quickly and with complete concentration. She would never throw any out. Checks that came, she would take and deposit somewhere in her little account. I used to laugh at this and thought it was cute, her squirreling away these little bits of my money. Fortunately, I was paid by direct deposit. Bills she would throw out. Fortunately, I had arranged for the majority of these to be paid via pre-authorized checking because I was out of town so much with work. Anything else she threw away unread.

Because I worried that she would throw away something important, I had gotten in the habit of checking the trash for unopened items of mail. One day, I saw a handwritten letter there, addressed to Shirlena but with a surname I had never heard. I opened it and read it in the light of the setting sun. "Hi Shirlena," it said, "You do not know me but I believe that you might be my birth mother..." and on it went. It was from a girl from some place up north. Way up north. It included a picture, a young woman in her late teens maybe. She looked like Shirlena. It was a high school graduation picture. The only thing that made me doubt the young woman's claim was her smile. I just could not imagine my Shirlena smiling like that. I just cannot see my Shirlena ever smiling. I kept the letter and the picture. I wanted to bring it up with her but could never think of a way. She gave me no chance to bring it up. She never talked about her past. By this time, we had ceased to talk about anything anyway. I never threw the letter or the picture away. I kept it in the glove box of the El Camino. Someday, I will go find the girl and tell her what I know, which isn't much and does not explain anything. I hope she will feel better. I think I will, too. Someday.

Or maybe I will just leave well enough alone.

I shut off the El Camino just before reaching the trailer and kill the lights so I can just roll on up. It's a '72; you can do that. You can't in a new vehicle where the lights come on with the engine. When I get out, I go to the front door and then decide fuck it, I am going in the back door. It's a bit of a jump, and I have to open the door first and swing up and in using the handle because of the missing steps, which isn't good for the door, but I am not getting a fire extinguisher anywhere near my vital organs ever again. I get in and the lights are off all through the trailer, except the flicker from the TV. Shirlena is watching TV in the living room. Old music videos. Retro. Not loud, but I can hear it. Strange to say, but I love the song that's on. It's some sort of a sign. So there she is, watching TV and smoking, smoking in my mother's trailer that had never been smoked in until Shirlena came. I walk on out in front of the TV. I do not stomp and rage, but I am not quiet. I lean back against the TV and fold my arms across my chest, but it's Shirlena who speaks first.

"I thought you were gone for good!"

I let her sit a minute before I respond. "Well, you thought wrong."

"Let me rephrase that," she says, "I hoped you were gone for good." Shirlena butts out the cigarette and sits up straight now.

"It's my place," I say. I stand up straight now, away from the TV, my arms still folded across my chest.

"I can fix that," she says. She gets up off of the couch now. She wears a T-shirt that comes to mid-thigh on her, and I bet nothing else. She just stands there. Acting "as if." She is not defying me, because I never give orders. She is used to being obeyed. We are quiet for a minute. I can't take this anymore. What can I say?

"YOU SHOULD NOT HAVE FUCKED WITH THE EL CAMINO!" is what I do say.

I point my finger and I spit the words and if I started with fury and dissipated within the space of a sentence at Tom's, I start with fury now and finish cruel and hard because I am going to be unforgiving now, unforgiving forever. I want it to be this way. This is it. This is fucking it. She knows it, too, and comes over from the couch, moving too quickly to speak and with every intention of smacking me across the side of the head with the palm of her right hand, but I catch her! I catch her! I catch her by the wrist with my own right hand and I am stronger than her, stronger and more powerful in my rage, I twist her arm behind her back and force her to the floor on her knees.

How do you like that, Shirlena?

"Go ahead and do it, you pussy!" she spits.

I push forward on her arm, leveraging my weight through her wrist against her shoulder to force her head down and on and she has to reach forward with her free hand to the couch to steady herself so that her face is not in the carpet, my mom's carpet, that now smells of cigarettes where it used to smell clean.

I want this much, Shirlena.

"Is that all you got?" she asks.

Her hand on the couch, she is now at length, and to stay upright she has to spread her knees for balance to avoid going over sidewise. With her knees that far apart, the T-shirt will roll up and expose her ass all round, her softness all wet, and she is a wounded thing and I am a killer. Her left hand is up on the couch and now my left hand is in her shirt to roll it up as far as it will go and when I am done, my left hand will find as much of her hair as it can hold, as much of that white stripe as I can hold, and I will lean back when I pull her hair, and I am over her and on top of her and into her and her head snaps back—snaps back hard—and her eyes are closed and she bites her lip to stop from making a sound. How do I know? I just know.

Give me this much, Shirlena.

"Are you a boy or a man?" she asks.

Her hand up on the couch and my hand in her hair—our postures are symmetrical—symmetrical in these gestures of people reaching. With our reach, our breathing intertwines, ragged and angry and hoarse. I am still over her and into her and I will not—I will not, I will not—stop—I will not stop—until she makes that sound. Her knees will be red from that unclean carpet. I have no idea how her scalp will feel but I bet it burns. It's when I think that, it's when I hope that it hurts, that she makes a sound. She makes *that* sound: she gasps and exhales, she pushes out some of her evil from deep within her and then, only then, at the close of that gasp, when she must breathe in again or die, I am called forth and my own issue comes from deep within me and it feels so fucking good, I think that I must be dying and dying I am happy and dying I am released.

Thank you, Shirlena.

She takes a deep breath and holds it for a bit.

"Your dick is like a baby's little toe," she croaks.

I do not let go of her hair right away. I let go when I have to, when I am released of the softness of her and when I am conscious of the pain in my own knees and I think of the mark it might leave upon me and the marks it will leave upon her. The last thing I do is let go of her hair, because I am thinking again and think to get back away from her, back off to the side where she might do me no harm.

And we are done.

I sit on the floor now, my back against the TV, my knees up to my chest where I can rub them. She pulls herself forward to get the top half of her body onto the couch after she rolls down the T-shirt again to cover herself up. She crosses her ankles again, her weight on the balls of her feet and her knees still, her balance less precarious because she rests on the couch with her arms and elbows crossed beneath her. For a moment, for a long moment, we just rest. The songs on the TV are still there, but not so loud. I don't look at her. I did not close the back door when I came in; it has swung open. I can hear the insects outside, swarming madly around the streetlights. So I look to them. They seem to spark with a fury born of an agitation they cannot possibly understand. I understand them now, when I am no longer possessed, now that I am weak again.

She gets up, and smoothes the T-shirt down with her hands to cover her nakedness. The gesture has no charm, no false modesty that a young woman might have. It's just a gesture born of thoughtless habit and she walks off into the kitchen, graceless and plodding.

"Do a shot with me?"

Her voice comes from the kitchen, but it's not a question. It's a statement and it's perfunctory. Back when she first moved in, we would often have a shot before—tequila always—she seemed to like it. I have no taste for tequila but I liked the ritual and the graceless love that used to follow it. But there has been no love lately. No tasting her mouth, the taste of the tequila, and the taste of her last cigarette and my mouth hard upon hers, demanding, not asking, and her yielding, begrudgingly like she begrudged me the air I breathed and me getting harder in my anger over this and me pulling her down and her finally yielding, yielding and making the sound like she always did and I felt like I had finally fucking won one. That was how it used to be, but not now. Now, I want the shot, I want her to leave, I want to leave, I still don't know.

"Bottoms up," she says when she comes back in, bearing the two shot glasses. I stand up and pull my pants up when she comes in, letting her hold the shots at arm's length. I still have my shirt on. Never took it off. Or my boots either, for that matter. I am damp. I make her wait while I get the shirt tucked in, and the belt done up, then I take it. I keep my eyes on hers at all times. I am going to pound back that shot and then tell her to get the fuck out, that's how I am going to do it. Shirlena pounds her shot.

"Don't you fucking look at me," she says

when she is done. Ah, Shirlena, she hates me still. She is like water; she yields only when she must, when she is displaced, and when she doesn't have to yield anymore, she comes back in and fills your space up again.

I never take my eyes off of hers when I raise the shot to my mouth, but something, I cannot say what it is, but I see something in her, something in her eyes makes me stop— stop close enough to smell it.

Bleach.

The shot is fucking bleach.

"For fuck's sakes, Shirlena—it's, it's...it's not even real poison!" I say, setting it down on top of the TV. "To hell with you! Be out of here by tomorrow morning. Just get the fuck out. I'm coming back with the Sheriff. If you are here, there will be hell to pay. Just take your bullshit act and get the fuck out!"

She says nothing. Just stares. Maybe it's my imagination, maybe it's the four beers, but I see her eyes and they can't hold mine anymore and I see her face and I think there is a bit of a Mona Lisa smile there.

Busted!

I walk on out. I have won. I walk on out the back door and forget about the steps so I hit the ground hard. Somewhere, I am cut, somewhere I bleed, but I bounce back up, I have won—I think.

I fire up the El Camino and peel on out. Fuck the neighbors, fuck the cops. I floor it. Damn! I think that I should have had that last beer. In the rearview mirror I look back and see her standing there in the back doorway. High above the trailer is the streetlight, surrounded by the burning corona of stinging insects. Unlike Thumper with the Baptist lady I am not even close to going back. I speed away, I exceed the limit, and I miss the lights and signs.

I am done with Shirlena. I do not know what to do now, but I don't need to worry about that. I am done with Shirlena.

Tom's will still be open.

I drive too fast now; I look for the lights and the signs but run them anyway. Let the cops bust me, if they are there. If not, I am gonna fly.

When I get to Tom's, I park in the lot across the street, in the row behind Johnny's

Camaro. The Camaro is still here, but that's no guarantee that he'll be here. Johnny is good about one thing: he won't drive the Camaro once he has had so much as one drink. A company truck—hell—he usually needs a six-pack to drive one. But not the Camaro. When I walk in, I see that Johnny and the whole crew are gone. Just Terri behind the bar and in front of it, one of those old fellers who play the video poker machines for a living and whose name only Terri would know. It's just after midnight.

"Hey Dan," Terri greets me, her voice soft as she condescends. "Problems solved?"

"Pepsi," is my answer. "Please." My mom raised me to be polite.

"Tell you what?" Terri says, "Let me make you a Reach-Around. Whiskey, gin and juice. Shaken. Strained. Poured on ice. They're the best. I love making them. It beats popping the top off of another beer. And Dan-O, you look like you could use a Reach-Around."

Terri's right, but "Pepsi" is still my answer. I need to think clearly, not get more messed up. Sugar, caffeine, and it's cold. What's not to like? So Pepsi it is, and I sit in silence. It is just Terri, the old video poker jockey at the other end of the bar, and me and my Pepsi in silence. And in the silence, the air grows heavy, and in its heaviness, it grows cool, and when it is cool, it lies still, and in the stillness, the sound of metal on the plastic veneer of red automotive paint from all the way across the parking lot comes to me and I recognize it like the song playing on the television when Shirlena and I parted company for ever and ever. And in the stillness and on that sound, in he walked for the first time.

I have told you of his appearance already. A thing of wonder, really and truly. I had to turn to see him, because he cast no reflection in the mirror behind the bar, although I could feel him standing behind me and beside me—standing over me as it were. Even though he was the smaller of us two.

"Who are you?" was all I could say. Stupid really.

"You know who I am." he says. His voice reveals certain affability. He did not condescend at all. It is just us talking, just us two.

"What do you want with me?" is all I can think of to ask. I am still mad and dumb with anger.

He laughs—gently. Maybe he is starting to condescend. He can't help it. "I want nothing with you, Danny," he says. "This is just a courtesy. I have come for Shirlena, come to take her with me. You will not see her again, nor will you see me. Do not let false pride swell up in you. Do not argue this thing. Do not contest this fate that I have made. There is no one to impress. We all understand. In the end, you will speak well of me."

"I have never asked for this."

Again he laughs. Maybe he can't control himself so well. And why should he? He is the Prince of Darkness. What am I—or what is Shirlena—to him? "Do what I will" is the whole of his law. "You don't have to ask, Danny," he says, "and don't think that it was you in the first place. There were lots of prayers for Shirlena, some going this way, some going that. We hear all prayers, He and I," and at this, he looked to the ceiling, "and in this case, I got here first. We are both busy, far too busy, but eventually one of us had to come. So the world goes round and round."

I have nothing to say, and so I say so.

"Nor should you," he says, and with that,

he walks on out into the stillness.

The old video poker jockey leans down the bar, sprawling with age, drunkenness, and the poor posture born of his hours before the poker machines. "That young feller," he says, gesturing with a lit cigarette held between two fingers and his voice crackling with whiskey and smoke, "that young feller cast no shadow." He raises his eyebrows and nods, as if I should know.

Well, I know.

"Who was that?" Terri asks, turning around to face the bar. She has made the Reach-Around, and sets it in front of me.

"Lucifer, the Prince of Darkness," I tell her the truth. What's the worst thing that will happen—she won't believe me?

"Oh yeah?" she says, "What'd he want with you, Dan-O?"

"He's come for Shirlena," I tell the truth again. It's like a compulsion now.

She laughs at that. And then she yells at the door "HEY, SATAN! MILLION DOLLAR MURRAY! HE NEVER TIPS. EVER!" and she laughs. She turns to me again and shrugs her shoulders, "If he'll answer your prayers, maybe he'll answer mine. Hey! I don't ask for much!"

I say nothing. It was not my prayer. And shit goddamn, it is the Prince of Darkness. I think that it is best not to make jests at this particular time, in this particular place. I think of the guy that died in here that one time, died in the can, and I wonder if his spirit is at rest or if it heard Satan's call. Odd, isn't it? That I should not fear Satan upon meeting him and that in his absence I have found not religion, but superstition.

"I think he keyed Johnny's Camaro," I say. I set my Pepsi down without finishing it. I get up and go outside to check on the El Camino. Walking across to the El Camino the only reminder of his malevolent presence in the unnatural stillness of the air. I look up at the streetlights; the insects that swarm and swirl about them seem to be frozen in place, as if they were the stars of some far distant galaxy. It is as if time has stopped. When I walk by the Camaro, I see the long thin scratch in it, a white scar in the red paint, like a negative image of a wound to the skin of a living man. Johnny's gonna be pissed. When I get to the El Camino,

I see no marks on it and I stand for a bit, just looking at it. Hey, I can do whatever I want now that Satan has solved all my problems. I think I'll paint it black. The thought of being asked why makes me smile. "Why'd you paint it black, Danny?" they will ask and I will answer with "All Hail Satan!" But I always liked black. I see it is unlocked and for the fuck of me I can't remember whether I locked it or not, but I am pretty sure I did. I open the door and slide on in. Faintly, faintly I smell bleach. It must have been on my hands from the incident at the trailer and now it is on the wheel. I look up at the halo of insects above the streetlight: a crown of thorns, a crown of lights, they wheel and spark now, moving and writhing and when one vanishes, lost into the night, two more take its place. The El Camino seems all right. I don't know why I think it, but I think it, and I open the glove compartment. Just to look. The letter from the girl, that girl that smiled so unlike my Shirlena—it's gone. Gone! I look on the floor but it's dark and I give up quickly. I know it's gone. I know it with the same certainty that I know my mother's love. But I can't understand why. Where at first I was unafraid and then I was a little afraid now I am just angry. Not as angry as I was at Shirlena when she handed me the shot of bleach. More like a sad anger. So this is how it ends. I cannot believe he would take that. How could he have known? What prayer could he have heard? What curse? But you know, I guess this is the way it has to be. That letter weighs heavier upon me than whatever happens to that bitch Shirlena. I smile when I think of that, too. When it ends it all ends at once. I get out of the El Camino and lock her up and walk back in to Texas Tom's to meet the Devil for the second time in the same night.

"Tiger Lily" was first published in Existere, Journal of Art & Literature; "The River by the Garden" in the Molotov Cocktail; "Flower" in the Molotov Cocktail; "One Inch of Air" in Tracer; "Black Dog" in Ginosko Literary Journal; "King of Diamonds, King of Hearts" in Minor Literature[s]; "Indolence and Rhyme" in Toasted Cheese; "Forty-Five Minutes of Unstoppable Rock" in Bull: Men's Fiction; "June 25th, 1977" in Bird's Thumb; "All of the Words to All of the Songs" in Chicago Literati; "Broke" in Sunstruck Magazine; and "Cold Enough to See Our Breath" in Across the Margin.

ACKNOWLEDGMENTS

This book would not have been possible without the unfailing encouragement and hard editorial work of the following people: Firstly Lori Hahnel, Minkee Robinson, Kevin Mulligan, Amy Whitmore, Kathy Doll, and Jeff Rosaine, Stacey Brandes Doss and Pamela Miller Wood, first readers extraordinaire, certainly Jerry Brennan, Jaime Harris, and Leanna Gruhn of Tortoise Books who made this all happen, and last but not least, my family: Guy Passey, Jane Passey, Zachary Passey and Matthew Passey. For everything you all have done: Thank You.

ABOUT THE AUTHOR

Steve Passey is a two-time Pushcart Prize nominee for fiction. His work has appeared in over fifty literary magazines both on-line and in print in Europe, Australia, South Africa, the UK, and North America. He is originally from Southern Alberta.

ABOUT TORTOISE BOOKS

Slow and steady wins in the end, but the book industry often focuses on the fast-seller. Tortoise Books is dedicated to finding and promoting quality authors who haven't yet found a niche in the marketplace—writers producing memorable and engaging works that will stand the test of time.

http://www.tortoisebooks.com/